More praise for *Whippoorwill*

★ "Narrator Clair is absolutely believable as the girl who's stable yet also negotiating her own loss." —*The Bulletin*, starred review

"Destined to become a classic. . . *Whippoorwill* is about the love and care and neglect and magical interspecies connections between an animal and members of a family, and it will both devastate and transform you. I love this book." —Luanne Rice, *New York Times* best-selling author of *The Lemon Orchard*

"*Whippoorwill* is an invitation to walk a mile in Wally's paws, and discover that sometimes there are strays of the human variety—and they, too, need love, compassion, and, most importantly, trust." —Jennifer Brown, author of *Torn Away*

"A sweet story about a lucky dog that reveals itself to be a deeper story about a lucky human." —*Kirkus Reviews*

★ "The narrative adeptly portrays longing and belonging, and the heartbreak and hope of not only the human condition but the canine one as well. Monninger revitalizes the boy-and-dog trope in this sweet novel." —*SLJ*, starred review

WHIPPOORWILL

BY JOSEPH MONNINGER

Houghton Mifflin Harcourt
Boston   New York

Copyright © 2015 by Joseph Monninger

www.hmhco.com
The text was set in Minister.

The Library of Congress Cataloging-in-Publication Data is available.

ISBN: 978-0-544-53123-9 hardcover
ISBN: 978-0-544-81356-4 paperback

Manufactured in the United States of America
DOC 10 9 8 7 6 5 4 3 2 1
4500611013

For my dog, Laika.
Last of the sled dogs.
No truer heart ever lived.

If people bring so much courage to this world the world has to kill them to break them, so of course it kills them. The world breaks everyone and afterward many are strong at the broken places. But those that will not break it kills. It kills the very good and the very gentle and the very brave impartially. If you are none of these you can be sure it will kill you too but there will be no special hurry.

—*A Farewell to Arms* by Ernest Hemingway

The quality of mercy is not strain'd,
It droppeth as the gentle rain from heaven
Upon the place beneath. It is twice blest:
It blesseth him that gives and him that takes.

—*The Merchant of Venice* by William Shakespeare

ONE

AT NIGHT I could always hear him.

He turned on his chain, trying to find a comfortable spot, and you heard a moment of quiet as if the whole world waited to see what he would do. Then the chain chinked just a little and you could hear him huff and then fall into his dog box, the heavy thump of his body on the boards, the chain lifting a notch to accommodate his neck.

Sometimes he whined and I could hardly stand it.

It turned minus thirty one night and he still stayed outside.

"It's New Hampshire and it's late February," my dad said. "What do you expect?"

He sat at the kitchen table fooling around with his motorcycle parts. He had his big beard then, his winter beard, and he hardly had cheeks for all the whiskers. He wore a quilted flannel shirt and red suspenders. A pair of tortoiseshell glasses from Walmart perched on the end of his nose so he could see one of the parts.

"He shouldn't be outside," I said, looking out the door at the porch thermometer.

"No, I guess not," he agreed, "but we can't start a war with the neighbors."

"The heck with them," I said. "I hate them. We shouldn't care about them if they can't bother to care about the dog."

"That's no way for a sixteen-year-old girl to talk, Clair. We can't judge other people so easily."

"He could die."

"All things die," he said, not looking my way.

He meant my mother, I knew, but he was being poetic.

That night, in the cold, I threw some leftover breakfast sausages to Wally. They landed close enough to his pole so that he could get them, but he didn't even respond. The snow had covered his back legs, and for a long time I stood watching, trying to tell if he had frozen to death. He looked back at me. His two nostrils streamed puffs of white air. White air, white night, white moon.

A black lab named Wally.

A dog is a social animal. Tying a dog out on a pole by himself is about the cruelest thing you can do to a canine. Dogs live in packs and some scientists say they care more about other members in their pack than they do about humans. They only care about humans if you become one of their pack.

Instead of tying a dog out by himself, it would be kinder to shoot him.

My bedroom looks out on the Stewarts' property. I could see over the stockade fence that separated our cruddy yards, and I watched Wally from the time he arrived in mid-February. The Stewarts are what people in New Hampshire call Whippoorwills. It's a north country name for trash hounds. The Stewarts have at least five cars in their backyard in various states of disrepair, two half-beat Farmall tractors, both spotted orange, a snowmobile so rusted, it looks like it wants to grow into the earth, an aboveground swimming pool that has collapsed on the north end so that it lies crushed and broken and useless, a trampoline that works, a stumpy white pine, at least five truck axles, and a dozen chicken pens, built above ground to house rabbits and a couple of guinea hens.

Wally was one more piece of junk.

* * *

We aren't much better.

My dad, John T. Taylor, is a wannabe biker. He has a Harley Softail, which, if you know anything about motorcycles, is supposed to be a big deal. He rides with a pack of guys called the Devil's Tongue, and they aren't as tough as they'd like to be, but they can intimidate the local New Hampshire people when they thunder up and down Route 25. You can feel them in the ground when they pass, and they always remind me of locusts or buffalo when I see them traveling. If you know who they are, though, they don't scare you a bit, because you understand my dad, for instance, is a heat and plumbing guy, and the Devil's Tongue leader is a little weirdo named Jebby. Jebby looks like a rhinoceros, all shoulders and neck, except he is only five foot four and pigeon-toed. Jebby is a rural mail carrier, which means he drives around on dirt roads shoving mail into boxes. He has a blinking light on his Jeep, and he eats turkey sandwiches at the same highway turnout every day of his working life at 12:10 sharp. That's where my dad sometimes finds him to talk about rides. The other guys are more or less the same, tradesmen and grease guys, and you can't be around them without understanding they sort of like the idea of being in a motorcycle gang, but they could never commit to being in a real one like the Hells Angels or the Iron Horsemen. After Mom died about three years ago, the motorcycle became more central in

my dad's life, and he's always working on it, one way or
the other, with the small kitchen television blasting and
the breakfast table covered with newspapers and machine
parts. Jebby comes by sometimes, and so do some of the
others, and what they seem to like most is *talking* about
riding. They rhapsodize about riding without helmets, and
about Bike Week in June down at the Weirs in Laconia,
New Hampshire, and part of me can't stand to listen to
their ridiculous talk, and another part of me is glad my
father has someone to talk to. He's kind of a loner—well,
we both are—and sometimes it feels like we are two dice
rattling around in this cruddy old house, and that when my
mom died, she gave us a great big shake and we've been
rolling ever since.

For what it's worth, my mom, Sylvia, was what people call
flighty, when they're being kind, and undependable, when
they're being mean. She was a part-time art teacher at
some of the elementary schools here in New Hampshire.
She drove around in an old Subaru station wagon and went
to different schools and worked with the kids. She special-
ized in found art. Found art is when you take old junk
and make something more interesting out of it. *The junk
suggests its shape to you,* she'd say. What that really meant
was the porch of our colonial house was so jammed with
crud, you could barely squeeze through it, but Mom didn't

notice. She was always going to yard sales or buying some cheap junk at Second Comings, the church secondhand store. It was a disease with her, really, like a hoarder who uses other people's discards to seal herself off from the world. Walling herself off, living way down inside herself, constituted my mom's real art.

TWO

WAS RAISED a Catholic, but I've only gone to Mass a couple times. I usually went when my mom was on some turn-over-a-new-leaf kick, but I remember Father Poloski saying one thing that stuck with me. He said you could commit a sin by doing wrong, a sin of *commission*, but you could also commit a sin by ignoring something wrong in front of you, a sin of *omission*.

Wally existed in front of us all, and I did nothing for about fourteen days. Maybe a little longer.

I suppose that's some kind of sin.

* * *

Here's what changed my life and made me approach Wally.

It was mid-March and lousy out, but the weather had turned warm enough to just melt the snow off most of the backyard. I sat in my room listening to music, or doing something stupid, and I'm not sure where my dad was. Maybe he was napping, I don't know. But when I happened to look outside, I saw Danny Stewart standing about two feet in front of Wally with some food. They fed Wally scraps, that's all, because they were too cheap, or broke, to buy kibbles, and normally they simply threw junk into a pail and dumped it out on the ground in front of him. On this day, though, Danny lobbed chunks of food at Wally and the food bounced off the dog's big head. Danny laughed and kept digging in the pail, throwing things in an arc toward the dog, and Wally looked around, dazed, the food bouncing off his head. Then Danny started pelting the dog with the food, throwing it as hard as he could, and Wally still thought they were playing. The dog looked up with an expectant expression, his tongue sideways in his mouth, and now and then he snuffled down and ate a piece of the food Danny threw. I couldn't stand the disconnect: Danny hitting the dog with such pure pleasure, and the dog receiving it as the only kindness he was likely to uncover in his endless isolation. If Wally had cowered, or whined, I might have been able to endure it, but the image of the dog hoping he had a playmate, or had at last a companion of some sort, killed me.

I tapped on the window. Danny looked up. He appeared to feel the tiniest bit guilty at being caught throwing food at the dog, but when he saw it was only me, he lifted his hand and shot me the bird. Danny was seventeen, and had his own car, and he thought he was cooler and worldlier than any of the other kids in the neighborhood. When I shook my head telling him to stop, he double pumped the bird at me. Then he dumped the rest of the food on the ground next to Wally and walked back inside.

I watched Wally afterward. He kept staring at the back door where Danny had entered the house. His eyes didn't move and he didn't bend down to get the food scattered around him. Food is one thing, attention is another.

Father Jasper was an old man, a semiretired priest, when he wrote a book with the simple title *My Pack*. He put into it everything he had learned about dogs over his seventy-eight years. He published it himself and gave it away free until a New York publisher discovered it and reissued it under the same title. Within three months of its commercial publication, it became a runaway bestseller. During the wave of its success, Father Jasper refused invitations from the media; he did not go on the usual television shows to promote the book, despite repeated requests and soaring sales. He released a simple publicity statement saying that he found in a dog's love the merciful acceptance he hoped to receive from God and from his fellow inhabitants of earth. Few photographs of him made it onto the Internet, but when they appeared, he always had a dog by his side.

With the money he earned from the book, he bought a hundred-acre tract of land in Maine, set up a school, and began teaching other people what they could learn from their dogs. He called it the Maine Academy for Dogs. People pay to bring their dogs for training. They live in spartan dormitories, train with their dogs seven days a week, and get to know their pets in an entirely new way. Father Jasper and his staff take homeless dogs off the streets around the country and train them to become exceptional pets for families. They sell the trained dogs to families who want an extraordinary pet. Also, dog lovers donate to the Maine Academy for Dogs because they want to sponsor good dog citizens.

I found his book, *My Pack,* in our school library and took it out and read it while I watched Wally.

When I first thought about freeing Wally, I told myself I could bring him to Father Jasper at the Maine Academy for Dogs and he would know what to do. You have to imagine a thing to make it begin.

After seeing Danny chuck food at Wally, I still didn't do anything. That's the truth. I could pretend I had a big, important moment of insight, but I didn't. I was afraid, for one thing. And I was lazy. At night, when he whined, I consoled myself that it wasn't my problem and there wasn't anything I could do. Even more despicable, I pretended that Wally didn't have it so bad. I pretended he would be okay, that the Stewarts sometimes came out to pet him (they didn't) and that his life, when you considered it, didn't seem all that terrible. I needed to tell myself that story. We tell ourselves a lot of stories, it seems to me.

But Wally was like water seeping into me, dripping little by little into my consciousness. It took almost to April before I acted on it.

Also, I was bored. More things happen out of boredom than most people want to admit. I had colored my hair purple earlier that afternoon, and I had spent more time than I care to confess looking at the results. Purple hair didn't really change much, I decided. I looked like a lilac or a bruised eye. I didn't look punky or cool. I looked like a dork who made a half-lame effort to look cool. I took a shower and tried to wash most of the dye out of my hair, but that only made it worse. When I stepped out of the tub, I gazed in the mirror and couldn't believe how I looked. A lot of times I can blame it all on our lousy bathroom lighting and the crummy medicine cabinet mirror, but when I wiped off the mirror with the edge of my towel, I couldn't believe the girl who looked back at me.

Uninteresting, I thought. I wasn't ugly and I wasn't pretty. I was plain. My nose had two dents where my glasses usually rested, and my chin, bony and too prominent, stuck out like a doorknob. I had an image of someone grabbing my chin and turning it like they wanted to open it, my whole head rolling on my shoulders at the pressure. My neck looked too thin to hold up my head, and my shoulders, where they stuck out over the towel, looked like someone should attach strings and turn me into a marionette. My features didn't do anything interesting. Whenever I was in a group photograph—which I hated—I disappeared. No one's eyes went to me. I wasn't even the last girl picked for dodge ball. I wasn't even *that* interesting. I was a human backdrop, a type of necessary neutral gauze against which other people might arrange themselves. Mousy. A girl Chevy. A boring four-door.

That was my state of mind the first time I met Wally. Wally changed that, though. Wally made me someone.

THREE

I KNOCKED ON the Stewarts' door at sunset. I did it before I had thought it through and had time to come up with a lot of objections, and suddenly I was there, my hand moving back and forth, the sound of a television blaring from inside. Right after I knocked, I turned away and started down their crummy front walk, figuring fate had decided not to answer me. I do that kind of mind game. I had almost started to loop over into our yard when the door opened and Mr. Stewart looked out.

"What?" was all he said.

Mr. Stewart was a big, ugly man, who always stripped out of his shirt at the first bit of warmth. As soon as the temperature climbed above fifty, you could see him around town in blue jeans, a thick cowboy belt, and no shirt. He seldom shaved or got a decent haircut, which left his chin white and stubbly and his hair and side-whiskers wild and translucent. He logged for the King Mill, and I could never be around him without thinking of wood chips and splinters.

"I wondered if I could walk your dog?" I asked, turning.

"You can take the effing dog," he said, and shut the door.

That easy.

I'm not sure what I thought it would be like, but I didn't expect to be afraid of Wally. He looked so pitiful from my bedroom window, so eager and happy to see anyone who approached, that I figured he would be a big marshmallow. And maybe he was, but when I first walked into the Stewarts' backyard and stood a few feet away from him, he looked nasty. For one thing, he hadn't been bathed in forever, and he had pooped everywhere. The poop had frozen and thawed and looked like river-bottom mud, and it made me nauseated to think about walking across it to get to Wally. The chain had worn the fur away from his neck, and the skin underneath appeared red and sore. I didn't know for sure, but I would have bet money he had been on a chain wherever he had lived before coming to the Stewarts'. He had crusties in his eyes and one of his front teeth had broken off, so that his mouth appeared slightly lopsided. Flies or fleas had gotten to his right ear, and it was mashed down where he had clawed at it, its droopy edge tucking in like a boxer's. Also, he was big. He had a huge chest and enormous paws, and because he hadn't eaten a decent meal in a long time, his ribs looked like ladders running down to his tail.

I squatted. That's what Father Jasper says to do. Lower your posture when you meet a dog. It makes you less intimidating.

"Hiya, boy," I said softly.

Even that little kindness was too much for him. He jumped up against his chain and tried to come to me. His front paws waved in front of him until the chain cut off his air, and he went back down onto his four feet, then jumped again, his chokes loud and insistent and the measure of his desire.

Father Jasper says dogs are all about status and posture. Everything is hierarchy and dominance. They pee on trees to mark them and that sets a bar. The next dog tries to cover it and to pee higher on the tree. It's the way dogs are. You have to understand that behavior if you hope to understand dogs.

"Are you lonely?" I whispered. "You going to take it easy if I come over there?"

He put his front paws down, danced, then went back to choking himself.

"Easy," I said, standing.

I didn't look down at the dog poop as I walked over to see him. His chain, I noticed, had swept a perfect circle in the mud and dead snow around his pole. The inside of his dog box had leaked and ice covered the bottom. He had lived on ice since he arrived.

"I'm sorry," I said, and I felt close to tears. "I'm so sorry."

I put my hand out carefully. Wally licked my fingers. He licked them like a crazy thing. I let him do what he wanted. At least, I figured, he wasn't biting or growling. As I stood next to him, though, I wondered about letting him off his leash. His head came up to my waist; standing, he could put his paws on my shoulders. He looked ratty and undependable and more than a little nuts.

"I should have brought you some food," I said, slowly moving my hand to pet him a little.

Wally raked at my hand with his paw. He did it softly, almost as if he couldn't believe someone had decided to pay attention to him. It reminded me of the game I played with my mom when I was a kid. One of you puts your hand down, then the other slaps on top of it, then you slide your hand out and go on top of that, and so on.

That's what Wally did to me whenever I moved. He was so afraid I would take my hand away that he tried to keep it there.

"I don't know if even Father Jasper could straighten you out," I whispered to him.

The sound of my voice got him wiggling and crazy. He backed away and rose up against the chain and choked himself hard. Underneath his collar, his neck had red sores and scabs and fresh blood.

"If I let you off your pole, will you behave?" I asked.

Then he did something that killed me. At the sound of my voice he sat down and cocked his head to one side, and I saw the puppy in him. I don't mean to say he *was* a puppy, because he wasn't. He was old and gnarly and spazzy, but he had been a puppy once and I saw it in him. I saw what he could have been, maybe, if he had had a different life. I saw that he had once wanted to play, and to be friends with humans, and that he had suffered and taken it and he had slept on ice. Despite all that, he still hoped for kindness, and I couldn't help it anymore. I started to cry and I moved closer and I put my arms around his neck.

* * *

He let me. He stayed still. I asked him to forgive me for not getting him earlier, for not bringing some kindness to him. I told him the whole thing: that I had ignored him, that I had lied to myself about his condition, that I had been lazy and selfish and as cruel as the Stewarts when you came right down to it. I told him he should never forgive me, but that I would try to do better now and that he had one friend in the world. I told him people could be good, too, and that Father Jasper would help me teach him how to behave like a dog should. I told him to keep his heart open.

Even as I said it, though, I felt my laziness, my inertia, try to creep in and undermine it. I wondered if I would really follow through. It was horrid to think about, because I knew it was true. Even as I swore it, I unswore it.

I pulled a leash out of my pocket. It wasn't a real leash, just a length of hemp rope with a carabiner tied to one end. I showed it to Wally.

"You ever been on a leash?" I asked him.

I knew what Father Jasper recommends: A dog should walk on the left and it should understand that being on the leash is not a time to play. If Wally knew anything about being on a leash, he didn't show me. He jumped up and put his nose against the carabiner and tried to smell it. I squatted just out of reach.

"I'm going to put you on here, but you have to promise to be calm," I said. "You hear me?"

Wally jumped up and choked himself some more.

Everything I did was stupid. I know that now, but I didn't know it then. Father Jasper would have told me to use a prong collar. On a big dog like Wally, a prong collar was the only way to slow him down. When a dog acts crazy and strains against the lead, a prong collar makes him uncomfortable by pinching and lets you get his attention. That may sound cruel, and it is a little, but it's one of the only ways to get through to a really nutty dog. The thing is, a dog that's never been socialized doesn't pay attention. It has no idea who you are or what you want from it. It's just *dog*, and you are other, and the collar and leash and the squawking human saying commands has no more meaning than the chirping birds or rain clouds.

Father Jasper says a trained dog is a free dog.

What people think of as a free dog—a dog without manners or socialization—usually ends up in a shelter or dead from a car knocking its guts out. Untrained dogs are just waiting to do something to get themselves killed or locked up. A trained dog is free because he has enough sense to come back when he's called, to stop when he's asked to stop, to stay when he's asked to stay. A trained dog can walk in the woods off leash and have a grand time, while an untrained dog has to yank and struggle against a leash until no one can stand it anymore.

I clipped on the rope and unhooked him from his pole chain.

I hate thinking about what happened next. He surprised me. In the instant he heard that chain drop away, he turned *toward* me, not *away* as I expected, and he tried to climb me. He shinnied right up my body, springing off his back legs, and I fell backwards and spun and rammed my spine into his pole. The pain killed. It hurt so bad, I couldn't even focus on it, and before I had a chance to sort anything out, Wally took off. He took *off.* He went from zero to a hundred in the length of the rope I had, and if I hadn't wrapped the end of the lead around my wrist, he would have been gone that second. Instead, the rope snapped taut and my shoulder nearly came out of its socket. The force of the snap made me jerk against the pole again, pinning my arm in such a way that Wally couldn't move except by breaking my arm. He jumped back again, delighted to have me on the ground at his level, and while he tried to lick my face, I crawled away from the slack and got my arm away from the pole, and then he really took off.

I slid through dog poo. I slid through mud and old food and more kinds of crud than I thought existed. At that point I didn't care what happened to Wally. I wanted my wrist free of the rope. I clanged off one of the Farmall tractors, and the momentary slack helped me get back onto my knees. Wally shot off in a different direction, running at right angles to the tractor, and I screamed at him. I cursed him a blue streak. I couldn't stand up, because each time I tried to get my weight under me, he yanked again, finding something new and ridiculous to sniff, and I attempted to get my legs out in front of me. That way, I figured, I might be able to pop up onto my feet if I had a chance to slide feet first, but thinking and doing were two different things. Wally dragged me again, this time toward the front of the house and the street, and I half hoped someone would look out of the Stewarts' house, even Danny, and run out to rescue me.

"Stop it, Wally," I said half a dozen times. I let my voice get loud so someone inside might hear me.

I remembered the blaring television, though, and I scrambled after Wally, trying to prevent him from jerking my arm out of its socket, trying not to slide into anything else. I finally wedged my knee against the base of a baby beech tree and I used the leverage to haul back on him.

I wanted to kill him right then.

That's not merely a figure of speech. I wanted to kill that dog. If someone had handed me a gun, I would have shot him and walked away without a second thought.

Even as I yanked at him, he managed to get his nose onto something new. He strained against me and I strained against him, and it wasn't the last tug of war we would have, but it was the fiercest. And then with his right paw he dug at something just out of reach of his muzzle and he pulled it back to him. I thought at first he had killed a rabbit or a mouse, because something squeaked horribly, and I couldn't believe he had managed to execute something so efficiently. He turned around to show me, and I used the moment to yank him closer and I almost didn't see the gentle look blossom in his eyes. He had found a copy of the Daily Growler, the rubberized squeak-toy newspaper people give to dogs, and I knew he had spent weeks, maybe three or four, waiting for the moment to get to the Growler. It had waited like some tender moment of play suspended for days in ice and wind and rain, alive only in his memory and forgotten by every other creature in the world except Wally.

FOUR

D ON'T YOU LOOK ravishing this evening?" Jebby said.

He had a Budweiser open in front of him, and he sat at the kitchen table beside my dad. Jebby did his rhino smile, smirky and dumb and grassy.

"What happened?" my dad said, looking up from a motorcycle part. He had been heating it with a little flame from a welding wand, and he held the flame away from him while he examined me.

"I tried to take Wally for a walk."

"The dog?" my dad asked, genuinely surprised.

"Yes."

"That dog's crazy," my dad said. "You're lucky he didn't attack you."

"By the look of her, maybe he did," Jebby said. "You smell something horrible."

"His yard is disgusting," I said. "There's poo everywhere."

"You okay?" my dad asked, and clicked off the burner. "Honey, what's going on here?"

I couldn't say. I felt like crying, but I didn't want to give Jebby the satisfaction. He used any sign of weakness by a girl as a tool against women all over the world. Mom had always called him a pig, but not a full-grown one. *Piglet,* she'd said. Meanwhile, my back felt as though it had a long scrape down near my belt line, and my shoulder clicked whenever I moved it. I knew I smelled bad. I wanted a shower, but I was afraid to touch anything on my way upstairs. I stood by the back door like a little kid in a snowsuit, hands out at my sides, paralyzed.

"Did the dog bite you, Clair?" Dad asked.

"No, it just got excited and wanted to play."

"That dog has some Dane in it too. Great Dane," Jebby said, turning his beer up to his rhino lips. "He's a horse."

"It's a decent dog," I said.

"Elwood Stewart is not a man to trifle with," Jebby said, referring to Wally's owner. "I remember one time down at the Homegrown Lounge he beat up two men in a bar fight. I mean, he was some fierce . . . There was another time—"

"You need help?" my dad asked, cutting him off because Jebby liked to talk about the past more than the present, and he would go on and on and my dad knew it.

I shook my head and went upstairs. My eyes got full once I went away from Jebby. In the bathroom I slowly peeled off my clothes in the tub. When I was down to my panties and bra, I stepped back out and filled the tub with water so it would take some of the filth off the clothes. I let the water slosh around on them for a long time. The steam from the hot water felt good on my face and pretty soon the bathroom warmed up. I felt drowsy and strange, almost as if I had come back from a long hike miles and miles away from my house. I couldn't let myself think too much about Wally. He had freaked me out. He was like a statue that had come to life and suddenly turned crazy alive. I never got to handle him or to know the first thing about him because he had gone so spazzy. I didn't really want to see him again.

Finally I took my clothes out and put them in a laundry basket by the hamper, and then I wedged the whole mess angled into the sink so it wouldn't drip all over the floor. I stripped down and stepped into the shower. I felt sorry for myself. I felt annoyed that my act of kindness had gone unrewarded and even unnoticed. I knew I was being small-minded, but I couldn't help it. That dog was genuinely ridiculous.

I showered a long time. I let the water run all over me. Nothing could have felt better.

Dad was in the hallway when I came out in a towel.

"You okay?" he asked. "I told Jebby to take off."

"You didn't have to do that. I'm okay."

"What do you say we go out for pizza, maybe? Just you and me. A little dad and daughter date?"

"You don't have to do all that. I'm fine."

"When's the last time we went to Ronnie's? Come on, I need to take the bike for a little spin anyway. Wake it up for the spring. It will give me an excuse."

"Do we have to go on the bike?"

"Sure we do. You're a Harley chick, aren't you?"

"I'm not a Harley chick, Dad."

"Come on. Humor me. I feel like I hardly see you."

"I'm here all the time."

He raised his eyebrows to ask again. I shrugged. I guess we agreed to go.

"Dress warm," he said. "It's still mud season."

"Then why don't we take the truck?" I asked as I closed the door to my room.

"Brrrruuuummmmm," he called back, making a motorcycle sound with his lips. Then he shifted into second. "Brummmmpppppp, brummmmmmmmmp."

Father Jasper says good and bad is a human construction placed on a dog's behavior. For instance, if you put a steak near the edge of a table and the dog slides it off and eats it in about three bites, that is good, or smart, behavior from the dog's point of view. It's natural behavior, actually. If we come in and say, *Bad dog, bad dog,* the words are meaningless to the dog, although he will decipher the tone of voice you use. A dog still thinks what he did was pretty smart, but he gradually learns that the alpha dog—you —doesn't permit that kind of thievery. So, if you're lucky, the dog will stop stealing meat off the table. Good and bad, though, have little to do with it. Dogs act on positive or negative reaction, that's all. Morality has nothing to do with it. There are a lot of humans like that, actually.

My dad drove easy on the way to Ronnie's. A couple times he slowed way down and looked forward, near the front wheel, and he bent and tried to figure out the meaning of a sound. It made me nervous when he leaned forward, because I had to lean with him, my butt perched on the back, my arms on my dad's shoulders. He didn't like what he was hearing, I could tell. It was a splatting sound inside the regular chunk of the Harley engine, and my dad had been fighting it for years. The sound was his White Whale, and wherever he went he asked different guys if they had a clue. He checked online, called Harley dealers all over the country, but he couldn't solve it. The sound didn't really do anything to the engine except make it a little less perfect than my dad would have liked, but it was the fleck of dust on an otherwise clear pair of sunglasses.

It was too bad he couldn't let the sound go, because the ride, I had to admit, was spectacular. We took Puddle Road, a backcountry route with fresh tar and a brilliant yellow line, and the bike held on like it was happy to be running. The stars had just started coming out and you could smell snow back up under the pines but the air tried to be warm and it stirred you up. Halfway to Ronnie's we stopped at the Pumpkin Span, a dinky bridge that went over two swampy areas, and the peepers called like mad. As soon as Dad turned off the bike, the clouds peeled back to let the moon filter down and it hit the water and you knew winter had passed again for another year and all the good, warm weather lay ahead. It was like the first day of vacation, and I crossed my arms across my chest and listened to the peepers and looked up at the half-moon.

"Some night," my dad said.

He had bent down to look at the front wheel but then had clicked his tongue against his teeth and stood.

"I'm glad we brought the bike," I said.

"Be cold on the way back."

"It will be worth it."

"Do you want a dog, Clair?" my dad asked, the confusion in his voice plain to hear.

"No, Dad, that's not it."

"What is it then?"

"I don't like that dog being left abandoned over there day in and day out."

"I know what you're saying. It's tricky, though, with neighbors. We have to live beside them."

"I know."

"Anything else we should talk about? I know I'm not always tuned in like I should be."

"No, Dad, everything's fine."

"You've never done anything like that before. Go over, I mean."

I didn't answer right away. I had to think about what I wanted to say, and even after I came up with it, I wasn't sure I should say it aloud.

"He was invisible," I said. "No one should be invisible."

What I meant to say was I felt invisible sometimes.

That was the truth, but I couldn't put it into words right at that moment.

"Maybe I could talk to Elwood," Dad said after he weighed what I'd said.

"Don't do anything. After today, I don't even know if I want to walk him anymore. He's seriously strong and seriously nuts."

"Okay," he said. "You getting hungry?"

"Yes."

"One thing, though, okay? Don't you ever tell me you're not a Harley chick. You're my Harley chick."

He put his arm around me and squeezed. A blue heron neither one of us had seen suddenly spread its wings and flew halfway across the second pond. It settled down without a splash and began wading, watching for frogs.

"Some night," Dad said again.

Stars. The sound of the bike and my dad leaning, leaning, the night flashing by. The taste of tomato sauce on my lips. Salt. My dad driving seriously now, cruising, taking pleasure in it. When we buzz past the Pumpkin Span, the peepers' calling explodes like a wave of sound, then falls behind us. A Doppler effect, I remember from science class. Then on a straightaway my dad reaches back and touches my knee. I bend forward and we rocket down the smooth blade of road. White birches pass like ladder rungs, and my dad does his yell, this crazy yodeling sound he does when he has the bike just right, the road just right, the everything just right. I yodel with him, and I feel self-conscious and dorky, but it's fun, too. It's going like nothing, and my dad throttles down to a normal speed in little hunks, the sound of the world returning in vibrations and tingles, and we might have been in space or under the sea for all the world coming back as it does.

FIVE

BEFORE SCHOOL the next morning I made a point of not looking over at Wally's yard. For one thing, the gouge on my belt line killed. It was bruised and red and as thick as a candy cane. I also didn't want to risk seeing him or having him see me. It was like spotting a homeless person on the street. You see, but you don't want to see. Seeing means you have to do something, and I had enough to occupy me with five classes and a social life from hell. In my head, Wally had forfeited his connection to me by his craziness the day before.

*   *   *

To get to school I had to walk three blocks to Riley's convenience store, then wait under the front overhang for the bus. I hated waiting at Riley's, because half the men in town showed up there to slurp coffee and complain. I swear that's all they did. They complained about taxes and the president, and they complained about gas prices and about anything new that happened in town. They critiqued road projects, or the crew going out to cut the electric lines free after a storm, or the new cook down at Annie McGee's Breakfast Buffet. I avoided going inside, but sometimes I had to, and whenever I did, I kept my eyes down and my body small.

On the morning after wrestling with Wally, I stayed against the building and waited for the bus and tried not to say anything to anyone. But Cal Ball (everyone called him Cow Bell), who had been in my class since kindergarten, insisted on telling me about a fight he had witnessed between Marilyn Summers and Ernie Caldwell at the peewee baseball game the night before. They had started off low, like a storm at a distance, but before long she was outside his pickup with a tire iron threatening to smash his windshield. Everyone rooted them on, according to Cow Bell, and the game didn't stop, exactly, but no one paid any attention to the players, and pretty soon Mr. Bushall and Mr. Tomkins went over and tried to intervene. Then

Marilyn Summers began screaming at them, and it wasn't until her son, J.P., left the game and ran over and sort of herded her back into their own pickup that she stopped screaming.

"J.P. deliberately ran into a kid from the other team and tried to fight him, like, an inning afterward," Cow Bell said, his breath smelling of cough drops. "It runs in families, don't you know?"

I looked at Cow Bell and shook my head. He wore his blond hair pushed up from both sides of his skull so that the two waves met in the middle and formed a ridge. He reminded me of a dinosaur, or a fish of some kind, and I simply shook my head and looked down at the ground. He wore camo clothes and boots that went up to his midcalf. He'd always worn camo and he'd always worn boots that went up to his calf. He was like one of those Russian dolls in reverse, with bigger and bigger versions of the same Cow Bell climbing out in the identical outfit each school year.

"Leave me alone, Cow Bell," I said.

"It does, you know? I read about it."

Then the bus pulled in and it was a few minutes late and I would have bet good money that the men inside mumbled over their Styrofoam cups that the driver, Lenny Parkins, was driving hung.

* * *

It was weird, but on the way to school I became aware of all the dogs I saw along the route. Some of them waited for the bus with moms or dads and a bunch of kids, living in their own little world around the people's feet, and others I spotted in the backyards on poles and lines and enclosures. I wondered how I had never noticed dogs before, at least in this way, and I thought of Father Jasper, and what he would say about each dog's situation, whether it was good or bad, fair to the dog, working to bring out the canine's best qualities. I hate to say it, but even with a quick glance you could see most people didn't have a clue about their dog's world. To them a dog was just another thing, like a barbecue grill or a fancy porch rocker, and it didn't mean that they didn't love the dog, it just meant they didn't recognize a dog for what it was and what it needed.

I wasn't an expert by any stretch, but simply looking critically at what was going on with people and dogs opened my eyes. I started writing little notes in my head to Father Jasper about what I observed. In the final analysis, that's what he preached: *Leave your people world for a second and see what it means to be a dog.* That was empathy, and it counted for dogs as much as it counted for people.

Cow Bell got shoved hard into the bus side by Larry Grieg as soon as we climbed down the stairs. Everyone laughed. Cow Bell laughed too, but I wasn't sure he thought it was as funny as the other people did. Larry Grieg was demented, and you had to laugh at whatever Larry Grieg did or risk making him go even crazier. His dad had died in a lumbering accident, and he told anyone who would listen that he was the man of the family now. No one believed it, of course, not even Larry himself, but you couldn't say anything without making him bull charge you if you were a boy, or flip an obscene gesture your way if you were a girl.

Anyway, the hard thing was watching Cow Bell. His camo was supposed to make him some sort of Marine tough guy, but it didn't give him the sawdust when it came right down to it. Larry Grieg unmasked him. When Cow Bell bounced off the bus, he laughed and kept his momentum going so he could drift away from Larry, and I knew without looking that he had a scared look on his face and a line of nervous sweat on his lip. I had known Cow Bell a long time, and now he knew himself.

Rumney High School. Home of the Catamounts, which is an old word for mountain lions. Purple and white are our colors. Our most famous graduate was a Civil War general who died from grapeshot—the guts inside a cannonball that fly out when it explodes—just as he mounted his horse. With his last breath he yelled, "Be true, boys!"

then he fell off his horse and died before anyone charged in either direction.

His name was Captain Earl Piedmont Rumney, and his last words were etched into a marble lintel above the main entrance.

His last words, though, didn't say anything to girls.

He came from our town more than our school, but the school adopted him as our founding father. We celebrate his birthday every May by playing a school-wide Ultimate Frisbee game that the football players take over and turn into an ape carnival.

I went in to see Mrs. Cummings. It was better to have someplace to go than to wander the halls and wait for an attack. Mrs. Cummings was not the lunch lady but the assistant lunch lady, and she had a tiny office—the old furnace room, actually—at the back of the school, where she caught a breath before starting all the chopping and peeling she had to do each day. She was a nice lady, the nicest, really, and we had become friends because she had known my mom back in the day. Way back. Mrs. Cummings had mostly gray hair now, and her skin had gone soft like a spotted pear, but if you spent time with her, you could tell she had been pretty once. She was short and still trim, but you could hardly see her figure because she wore an elephant-gray cardigan every day. The cardigan had big, baggy pockets where she kept her Tic Tacs, and her memory pad. Her memory pad was just a small notepad, brown and rusty colored, with white pages and blue lines. Sometimes she wore the memory pad rubber-banded to her forearm, and sometimes it stayed in her pocket, but it was always with her. It was where she kept her reminders and her shopping lists, plus a garden design layout that she had been working on for more than a year. She wanted a garden of daylilies, just daylilies, but varieties of every color ever created. She lived in a doublewide with Mr. Cummings, who was a long-distance trucker, and her plot wasn't big enough to garden. Still, she had dreams about the garden, and I liked sitting with her in the early morning, her door open to whatever weather had arrived the night before.

"There you are," she said when I arrived. "Just about gave up on you. You're running late this morning."

She was drinking tea. She had her memory pad flattened on the table in front of her.

"The bus was late. We almost didn't make it."

"Was Lenny hung?"

I shrugged and sat down on the turned-over five-gallon bucket she used as a footstool. I dropped my backpack between my feet and let myself settle. It always felt good to be in Mrs. Cummings's office.

"Well, he probably was. The town ought to fire him, and I don't say that lightly. Employment is hard enough to come by, don't I know."

"He was okay," I said.

She shook her head.

"Pink Charmer," she said, lifting the memory book to show me the addition she had made to her garden design. "I just saw it in one of my catalogs. It's a beauty."

"Pink, obviously, right?"

She nodded.

"Pink Charmer, then the blue one I like," she said, and bent close to read her handwriting. "Blue Summer Daylily."

"Pretty."

She sighed and closed the book. She didn't say anything for a second.

"Gosh, you look more and more like your mom every day," she said. "I mean it. Spitting image and all that. You must see it yourself."

"I guess," I said. "We don't have that many pictures of her around."

"Trust me," she said.

First bell rang. It rang loud and hard.

"Up and at 'em," she said when the bell died off.

She put her memory book under the rubber band

against her forearm. She dug in her pocket and shook a few Tic Tacs into her palm, then she held them out to me, offering.

"I'm okay," I said, "unless you're telling me I need them."

She laughed and shook her head. Then she slapped the mints in her mouth, and her hand cupped against her lips made a small popping sound.

When I came home at four, the spring light made me step out on the porch as I peeled a clementine. If you've never spent a winter in northern New England, then you don't know what spring fever feels like. You spend all winter waiting for a little warmth, a little sunlight, and when it returns, it's overpowering. But the warmth also melts the ice and snow, and whatever you left outside in December is still there, waiting, like a snapshot of your life. Everything is dirty and cruddy. I slipped my hip up on the porch railing and looked around our yard. Seriously, it wasn't much better than the Stewarts' next door. We had a broken umbrella-shaped clothesline and a cement three-step staircase broken off and resting on its side and a coffin-shaped bathtub filled with beanpoles and garden junk. Weeds poked up everywhere, not growing, but giving the place a graveyard air. The whole thing looked ridiculous, looked like whippoorwills lived here, and I hated thinking how accurate that was. I put a tiny piece of the clemintine peel under my front lip. It tasted bitter and harsh, but I wanted that, wanted to taste the light in the fruit, and I leaned out a little and put my face back into the sun. Then I took a big bite out of a fruit section, and it tasted like spring, and like summer later on, and I had a warm, floaty moment until I heard Wally whining.

Ignore him, I thought.

He kept whining, though, and I thought of him grabbing that Daily Growler, and thought of his paw swiping at my hand in a gentle way, and I tried to figure out what Father Jasper would do. He would call it a sin to ignore the dog, I guessed. So I shoved more of the clementine into my mouth and grabbed the lead from where I had left it on the porch the other day and I went around the stockade fence.

Wally went up on his chain, dangling his feet and trying to roll his paws like a horse rolls its hooves, and I looked at him for a ten count before I realized what had changed.

His yard had been raked. Not just raked, but really cleaned. He had a new water dish and he had kibbles in his bowl and even his house—a junky thing no matter how you sliced it—had been knocked together a little with extra pieces of board so that it appeared more solid. Someone had put a bag of grass clippings inside as a bed.

"What's going on over here?" I asked Wally, raising my voice a little like people do with dogs and children.

He put his front feet down, spun, and barked. I walked closer. To my astonishment, he also looked bathed. His fur glistened in the spring sunshine and his teeth looked better, his eyes brighter. The whole thing didn't feel so depressing.

My father, I thought.

I walked over and knelt down just within reach, but not close enough so he could maul me. He spazzed and chucked his head against me. In the entire world, the only thing that dog cared about was keeping me right where I was.

His fur felt warm when I touched it.

"Oh, you good boy," I said. "You good boy. Who was nice to you? Was it my dad? Did someone come over and clean you up?"

I was still petting Wally when Danny Stewart came out the back door.

"He looks better, right?" Danny asked.

No introduction, no hello, no how are you, no what's new? He simply walked out and started talking. He wore a sweatshirt with a picture of a black guy smoking a cigarette. The smoke trailed up over his shoulder. Underneath the picture a blue script said ALL ABOUT THE BLUES. For the first time I noticed Danny's sideburns had grown out. They were long and shaped like two snow shovels on either side of his head. I couldn't tell what look he was going for. It was half greaser, half rockabilly, but it made him more interesting.

"You did this?" I asked.

"I only go half days to the tech. I saw you out here before. It would have been funny if it hadn't been so sad."

"It wouldn't have been funny if you had kept the dog decently to begin with."

"It's not a perfect world."

"It can be a better world."

"I thought you'd be happy," he said, and came over and let Wally jump up on him.

Wally stood with his paws over Danny's shoulders. Wally was a really big dog.

"You shouldn't let him do that," I said. "It teaches him that it's okay."

"It is okay."

Danny rubbed Wally's ribs.

"It makes him impossible for other people to be around. He'll jump all over them. You have to train a dog."

"You train him if you want him to behave so much. He's okay with me."

"He's your dog."

"Look, my dad took him in payment for a job. The dog crapped everywhere in the house and ate everything he looked at. Dad was going to take him to the pound, but I talked him out of it."

"He'd have a better chance at the pound."

"Man, you know just about everything, don't you? You get nosebleeds sitting up there in judgment?"

"Just simple facts."

"Anyway," Danny said, pushing Wally down, "I admit he needed cleaning up. So I did that. I thought you might like it."

"I do. I do like it. I'm glad you did it."

"He's a nice dog. He doesn't mean any harm. He's just big and stupid."

"He's not stupid. Every dog is as smart as the people who own him," I said, quoting what I thought Father Jasper would say.

"Sit, Wally," Danny said.

Wally sat. He trembled as he sat, ready to go. I moved closer and ran my hand over his chest and shoulders and finally his head.

"They say you should pet a dog's body as much as its head. Everyone just wants to pet a dog's head," I said. "You wouldn't like it if that's all anyone petted on you."

"I might," Danny said.

He squatted down next to me. We both petted Wally.

"Who's 'they'?" Danny asked.

"A guy named Father Jasper and his staff. They raise dogs. He's a retired priest and he founded the Maine Academy for Dogs."

"Seriously?"

"Can we put him on the lead for a second?"

Danny shrugged, then took the rope from me. I stepped back. Danny put two hands on the rope as soon as he dropped the chain connector. Wally began pulling him around like a man on skis. But Danny kept his feet and let Wally move around. Wally marked half a dozen places with urine. His nose made a snuffling sound everywhere he went. Watching him, I thought Jebby was wrong about the Great Dane part. Wally had some bloodhound in him. His nose and muzzle flubbered when he sniffed at the ground.

"Can you make him sit on command?" I asked.

"Not really," Danny said. "Sometimes."

"Try."

Danny jerked the line tight and said, "Sit."

Wally paid no attention. Danny did it again, and this time Wally genuflected, and then kept going.

"He needs a lot of work," I said.

"I'm going to put him back now. You want to hook him while I hold him?"

I did. Wally jumped up on me and I shoved him off.

45

"Off," I said.

Wally slid off, then jumped again. I shoved him away again.

"You should knee him when he jumps," I said. "Not too hard, but you have to make it uncomfortable for him. You can squeeze his paws too. Dogs are protective about their paws, because if a dog injures his feet in the wild, he's a goner."

"Is this the priest guy telling you this stuff?"

I nodded.

Danny stood still until Wally jumped up on him.

"Off," Danny said, and kneed Wally in the ribs.

Wally went back to all fours.

"You want to go get a burger?" Danny asked, his hands running around on Wally. "I'm going out for a burger if you want to come."

"Where?"

"Smitty's. It's up in North Haverhill."

It was such a bizarre question, I didn't know what to say. I squatted next to Wally and petted him.

"Sure," I said. "I guess."

My stomach turned and vibrated and I thought I would throw up as soon as I said yes. I didn't know why I said yes, but I did. It would have seemed weird to say no, because we had just finished with Wally. Luckily, we both continued petting the dog, giving more attention to the task than it deserved. I asked myself a series of stupid questions, but the main thing that kept going through my head was *Danny Stewart?*

Not in a million years did I think of Danny Stewart as someone to date.

And was it a date? I couldn't even be sure of that.

"You're saying right now?" I asked, because I wasn't clear on what he was proposing.

"Yeah. You should probably grab a sweater or something."

"Let me run inside and leave a note for my dad. We won't be back late, will we?"

"Maybe I'll kidnap you," he said. "Ever think of that?"

"That's a weird thing to say."

"I'm just playing. Go ahead. I'm going to clean up. I'll meet you back here in a minute."

Danny Stewart, I thought as I walked back to our house. *Danny Jerk-face Stewart.*

My hand shook when I wrote a note for my dad.

Grabbing a hamburger with Danny Stewart. Up at Smitty's in North Haverhill. Won't be late.

I made a heart and signed my name. Dad would know, as well as I did, that what I left out of the note was way bigger than what I had put in it. Like: What in the world was I doing with Danny Stewart? Like: Who said I had permission to drive around with boys? Like: Who even knew I could date anyone?

By leaving things out, by being casual about it, I had made the note much more dramatic than I intended. It was not a big deal, I wanted to say. But saying it was not a big deal was a way to make it a big deal, so I kept it short and sweet and taped it to the handle of the fridge, where he was sure to go about thirty seconds after he made it home. I didn't look forward to the discussion we would have when I returned.

I ran back upstairs and looked at myself in the mirror one last time. Then I sprayed a little bit of perfume —Beautiful by Estée Lauder, my mom's big bottle that I took after she died—into the air and walked through it. Mom always said that was the way to put on perfume.

Danny Stewart?

What was up with those sideburns? I wondered as I came downstairs. And a sweatshirt about the blues? All I knew about Danny Stewart was that he went to the vo-tech, studied cars or diesel mechanics or something, had a maniac for a father, had a mother who sat at her kitchen table chain-smoking for a bunch of years before taking off to parts unknown, and had an uncle somewhere down south. The end.

I also knew he chucked food at Wally. And then cleaned him up. Too strange.

He stood next to the stockade fence when I came back.

"You smell good," he said.

"Just soap."

"I hope you're hungry, because they make big burgers up at Smitty's. You ever had one?"

"No."

"Well, they're something. Come on."

Wally barked when we left. The sun fell on his black fur and you could see rainbow colors if you looked hard enough.

SIX

HIS CAR WAS NICE. I had to give him that, although you also saw that it was a major big deal to him, and that kind of undermined it. It was a Chevy with the rear end raised up, like some boys like, and it smelled of wax and soap and ammonia. He had put a hula dancer on the top of the dash, and a pair of fuzzy dice on the rearview mirror, and those things inked a kind of thin line in my mind where I couldn't say if they were cool or complete jerk behavior, because I didn't know how he intended them.

He drove hard. Not fast, necessarily, but hard, revving the engine when he could and jamming the brakes when we came to a stop. He wanted to show off, obviously, but he also seemed to think the car needed to be handled that way, and I'd been around my dad and his Harley enough not to think it was completely idiotic. I stared straight ahead and watched him driving from the corner of my eye, and I felt about a million volts of weirdness charging around in my chest. For one thing, he had a really good sound system in the car that he hooked his phone into. He played the blues, exclusively, from what I could tell, but I had a hard time connecting the dots between Danny Stewart, jerk-to-the-ten-millionth-power, and this sort of cool kid slouched behind the steering wheel, listening to blues and driving his muscle car and raking up after his dog.

Also, the sideburns.

I couldn't get over the sideburns. I had known Danny Stewart a long time, almost since we were in kindergarten, and he had not done one cool thing, not even remotely, until he had grown out the sideburns. Driving with him, glancing over in quick bites from time to time, I saw he had a lot of red in his hair, and the sideburns collected most of it. It looked like his hair had leaked color into his sideburns, and they had spread out like two river deltas on either side of his head.

"You into the blues?" I asked, because you couldn't drive around in silence all the way up to North Haverhill and back.

"Bigtime," he said.

"How come?"

He shrugged.

"I mean," I said, "is there a reason? Why the blues and not something else?"

"Why anything? Who knows why? I like the music, that's all. And the bluesmen are pretty cool."

"Did your dad turn you on to them?"

Danny looked over.

"My dad is a jackass," he said.

"Sorry."

"Nothing to be sorry about. It's just the way it is, that's all. Some people get decent parents, some don't, and some get no parents at all. Mine's a jackass."

"Where'd your mom go?" I asked, although I had some ideas and had heard some rumors about violence and hitting.

"She left. No big deal."

"We both live with single dads then. That's weird."

"I guess that's true. I hadn't thought of it like that."

"Funny the way things work out."

"I wouldn't call our home life working out exactly. Would you?"

"My dad's okay."

"He's a big Harley man. I respect that."

He came to a straightaway and shot past a slow-moving pickup. I imagined I was supposed to ask about the engine under the hood, but I couldn't come up with a good reason to care. My stomach felt queasy anyway. It was strange having Danny driving, the blues coming through his sound system, the spring landscape pulling at something in my heart. Everything felt sideways, like we were two priests talking through the confessional boxes, both of us staring ahead. I had a hard time figuring out how Danny and I had lived side by side for so long and still knew next to nothing about the other person. My English teacher, Mrs. Philipone, would have found a metaphor about the human condition in that circumstance, but I couldn't make my mind go there.

Eventually he pulled into Smitty's. It wasn't much of a place from the looks of it. It had one large window in the center of the front wall, and down at the bottom the window had a hairline crack. I followed him inside. He didn't hold the door for me, but he pushed through first and sort of turned back to make sure I had made it, then he walked right to the counter. The odor of grease turned my stomach.

"I like the General Lee," Danny said. "It comes with onions, though, so if you don't like onions you probably don't want the General Lee."

"I might just have fries."

"Oh, you've got to have a burger. That's why we drove up here."

"Maybe a kid's size," I said, trying to make my eyes read the menu board. I felt jumpy and frazzled. I didn't want to stuff my face in front of him.

A girl came over and took his order. He turned and looked at me, waiting. I ordered a Kid's Classic, which was about the smallest thing on the menu. We both ordered Cokes. Then he walked over to a linoleum-topped table and sat down. I followed. The girl who took our order said she would call us when our food was ready.

An old couple sat at the only other occupied table. They ate without talking. The restaurant was partial to country western music, because we heard a twangy song start while we sat. I knew the song, but I didn't know who sang it. It was all about girls stepping out on a Saturday night.

"So, you think it's crazy that we're sitting here?" Danny asked. "I mean, you know, the way we grew up next to each other?"

"I don't know if it's crazy. It's a little strange."

"You never thought much of me."

"I don't know if that's fair to say."

"Oh, it's fair to say," he said, and laughed. "You liked looking down your nose at me."

"I didn't know you."

"You didn't care to know me. That's the truth. You put me over in a little box and you figured that was all you needed to find out about me."

"Danny, you've always been a jerk around the neighborhood."

He looked at me, then smiled. Then he laughed. It was a good laugh.

"You're probably right," he said. "Don't spare my feelings."

"You just were," I said, feeling the tension I had held in all evening come bubbling up. "You annoyed a lot of people, not just me. Sorry, but you asked. Besides, you didn't like me, either."

"My dad always called you Apple Annie," Danny said. "You used to eat apples all the time, so that's what he called you."

"That's ridiculous."

"It was just a name he gave you," Danny said. "Don't sweat it."

"What are we doing here?" I asked.

"We're getting a hamburger, that's all. Is there a law against it?"

"I mean, why did you ask me to come out here?"

"Because you're hot."

"I am so not hot," I said, blushing.

"Depends who's looking. I think you are."

"This is ridiculous."

Danny raised his eyebrows. He had gray eyes, slightly closed lidded, like a cat waking from a nap. I liked watching his face, I realized. He had an expressive face. It was almost like he was acting, but he wasn't acting, so it was okay. I couldn't make my mind push past the notion that he thought I was hot. No, I reminded myself, he *said* I was hot, but that didn't amount to a hill of beans. Guys said anything to girls. They just did.

Fortunately, the counter girl called us up for our food before we could go any deeper into things. I went up with Danny, and he paid. I didn't know if that made it a date or not, but I supposed it did. He had a wallet made of duct tape, I noticed. It was gray and sleek. He slid it back into his pocket and held the tray in front of him on the way back. He told me to grab ketchup and some napkins from a counter. I did. We slid back into the booth just as the music changed. It was still country western, but it was a guy singing about loyalty and horses and something about a pickup.

"Thank you," I said when Danny slid my plate off the tray.

"You're welcome. They have buffalo burgers you should try sometimes. They taste pretty good and they're supposed to be better for you."

"How'd you find out about this place?"

"Oh, I don't spend much time at home if I can help it. Not exactly a fun, family environment."

He smiled. It was a joke, I realized. Then he bit into his hamburger. It was big and he had to hold it between his hands like someone playing an enormous harmonica. A little juice dripped back on his plate. At least he kept his mouth closed when he chewed.

I took a bite. It was good.

"What I like to do," Danny said, referring back to how he had found out about the place, although at first I didn't follow his train of thought, "is drive. I don't know why. I like driving, and I like working on my car, and it's just feeling good with the window down. Maybe it's a boy thing, I don't know. But I go on little trips and get myself lost, and then I try to figure out how to get home, and how things are laid out. I have a gazetteer under the passenger seat and it has these maps all blown up so you can see the countryside, and I like pulling that out and comparing the roads to where I am and seeing the landmarks. You know, if you pay attention, you can see why things were built the way they were. Like, why did they put in a railroad here, down by the river, and then you realize, well, they had to follow the river because that's the natural way for the valley to run. I mean, it's not like they were going to put a train over a mountain, right?"

"I guess not," I said, watching him eat three fries.

"So then you can figure out patterns. If you simply drive along in a car and don't pay any attention, then it's just roads going around and around and back and forth. But someone plans those roads, and that sort of interests me. I talked to my vo-tech teacher, Mr. Allan, and he said that's all surveying and engineering, and he said, when you think about it, roads are parts of a motor, and if you could step back and see, then the entire U.S. is one big car of roads and airports and railroads. Do you see what I mean? You're not eating."

I took another bite and then ate some fries.

"I see what you mean, I think," I said.

"Probably a strange way to look at the world."

"Not really," I said. "It sounds like you think like an engineer."

"Maybe. I like taking things apart. Anyway, that's what I do. I drive around and see things, try to figure out how they work. And I stop for food now and then and I had always heard about Smitty's, so that's that."

"Why the sideburns?" I asked, and the question was out of my mouth before I could pull it back.

He touched his finger to his left sideburn and smiled. It was a funny smile, a smile that made you realize he was in on the joke and didn't take it too seriously.

"Why not?" he asked. "You don't like them?"

"I do like them. I guess I do. I hadn't noticed them before."

"They're supposed to match the side vents of my car," he said. "Like tail fins. I like the 1950s."

"You're weird, Danny."

"You're just getting that now?"

He was sweet on the way back, not hard-charging the way he was on the drive up, and he put his arm out the window and drove with one hand and he played the blues for me. He said the blues reminded him of rivers, that's the way it was, and the blues players understood about pain and loss, but they made something out of it. He said they spun gold from straw, which was a bit much, was like a line he practiced, but I listened anyway. And the music played over the good sound system, and it squealed and squawked, and cried at its own pain, accepting it for what it was, and I liked that Danny's hand beat with it on the side of the car sometimes, as if he couldn't get enough of it, as if it entered his body and had to come out somewhere, and it did come out through his fingers and he discharged it toward the ground outside like electricity, like tiny lightning bolts that passed through him.

I kept thinking, *Is this a date, is this* really *a date, and is he going to try to kiss me?* I thought yes, and I thought no, and

I thought about how Danny reminded me of Wally, both of them left to their own devices, and how maybe I was like a Daily Growler that Danny had wanted but couldn't reach, not sexually, not like that, but like proof of another person in the world, proof that someone else paid attention to him.

"You want to walk Wally?" Danny asked when we pulled back in his driveway.

"I do," I said, glad to have the distraction, glad not to have to think about kissing him one way or the other. "But I should tell my dad where I am."

"Okay, I'll meet you out at Wally's post."

"Thanks for the hamburger."

"My pleasure," he said, although he said it *plais-ir,* like French, like it should rhyme with brassiere.

I hurried through the Stewarts' yard and then hustled up the stairs to our kitchen. Dad wasn't there, but he had left a note where I had left mine.

Gone to Jebby's for a part. Back soon. Hamburger? Smitty's? Danny Stewart?

He had underlined "Danny Stewart" about five times. I couldn't blame him.

SEVEN

WHAT WE FIND in a dog is what we bring to a dog.
That's what Father Jasper says.

I felt a little sick walking over to Wally, and excited, too.
With my luck I knew Dad would return right when I was
over with Danny, and then we would all undergo an awkward, crazy moment or two while Danny and Dad tried to
figure each other out. Dad would have to see Danny *that*
way, as a suitor, or at least as a boy marginally interested
in his daughter, and Danny would have to see Dad as *Dad*,
an old bearded Harley guy, who maybe wanted to stick up
for his daughter.

All of that was possible. And it was also possible Danny simply wanted to go for a hamburger and I was around so he asked me.

I couldn't think it through too much. I saw Danny playing with Wally when I came around the stockade fence that separated our two yards. He had Wally dancing around off the post. I heard the Daily Growler squeaking, and Danny's voice was high and happy, saying things like "thataboy," "thereyougo," "thatsit." He was probably doing what Father Jasper wouldn't want him to do, getting Wally crazy and associating human companionship only with play, but I didn't have the heart to tell him. Danny looked kind of good in the late-evening light, kind of young and happy, and the same way I had seen the puppy in Wally, I now saw the puppy in Danny. He looked like he did before the sideburns, before the jacked-up car and bluesmen, looked like the kid I had occasionally glimpsed in our neighborhood. Cute, sort of.

"Hey," I said, coming around, letting him know I was there.

"Look at this good boy," Danny said, dancing around with Wally.

"He's a nice dog."

"He's a great dog," Danny said, bouncing around with him.

I crossed my arms. It was cold now. All the shadows

were long and tired. The sun had gone behind the mountains in Vermont, and one big shadow spread slowly across New Hampshire.

"I should do some homework," I said.

"Wait, tell me what this priest guy says. How do you train him?"

"I'm no expert. I just read the book. It's pretty good. It gives you a lot of common-sense tips, but it also talks about what a dog's spirit needs."

"I'd like to read that book. Could I borrow it?"

Part of me wanted to say, *You know how to read?* But I nodded.

"First of all," I said, coming forward and petting Wally, "when a dog's on a leash, he has to mean business. You can't let him pull and jump and go nutty while he's on a leash."

"How do you play with him then?"

"Well, you can play with him, but only after you've released him. In other words, he has to know when he's supposed to be serious and when he's supposed to play. The whole thing about dogs, Father Jasper says, is giving a dog something to do. Dogs want direction, they want a pack leader. If you leave a dog to its own devices, then it doesn't know what to do so it spazzes."

"Okay," Danny said, "so what do we do?"

I didn't really know. But I took the leash and put

Wally in front of me. He jumped and I kneed him off. I spotted a glimmer, just a glimmer, of a small change in his eyes. He understood we wanted to help him, to be with him, and so he didn't act quite as frantic as he had the other times I'd been around him.

"Sit, Wally," I said, and raised the leash.

He didn't sit.

"You only give a command once," I told Danny. "Father Jasper insists on that. If you say things more than once, then the command becomes sit, sit, sit, sit, and the dog doesn't take it seriously."

I put my hand on Wally's rear end, lifted the leash higher, and seesawed him into a sit. Wally popped right out, but I made him sit again three times. He got better each time.

"We need to give him biscuits when he does it right," I said. "Positive reinforcement. No punishment."

"Cool."

"You can bake your own biscuits. They're really cheap to make. I could make some if you're serious about training him."

"Sure, why not?"

"He could really be a good dog," I said. "I mean, if you worked with him. He's got a good heart. He's just never been told what's expected of him."

"You really think he could be a dog? A real, I don't know, a dog friend kind of thing? I always thought once something was set one way, it usually stayed that way. It feels like it is with most people."

"Of course he could. He's a good boy. Father Jasper is all about changing people and dogs."

"I'd like to borrow that book. I feel awful now knowing I didn't pay more attention to him. Seems kind of rotten."

I ran back to get the book. My dad was just pulling in the driveway in his truck when I came downstairs.

"Hey, where you going?" he asked.

"BRB," I said, which was a little code we used for "be right back."

"Okay, but don't go anywhere else."

"I'm just giving Danny this book about dogs."

"The priest book, huh? Okay."

Danny had Wally on the post by the time I got back. He had cleaned up a few messes and gave Wally fresh water.

"My dad's home," I said. "I should get inside."

"Okay."

"The book makes a lot of sense. If you read it in small doses, I mean, it makes sense. You have to be consistent with a dog, that's all. It takes time, though."

"Maybe you'd help me," Danny said, thumbing through the first pages. "Wild. He's a priest and he trains dogs?"

"That's what I said. I guess he had a temporary eye problem and he got used to a Seeing Eye dog being around. When his eyes got better, he still wanted to have a dog near him. Then he started to realize dogs had something to teach him. He talks a lot about love and acceptance. Some of the book is about his childhood and the dog he had then. It was a little beagle named Porky."

"I guess I didn't get who he was. Okay, it makes sense now. I'll read it tonight. It's like a car manual, right?"

"I guess you could say that."

I gave Wally a hug. He sat still and let me do it, which was a small miracle. Then I almost, *almost* felt like I should give Danny a hug. Instead, I backed awkwardly away, raising my hand in a stupid little wave.

"See you, Danny. Thanks again for the hamburger."

"You're welcome. Thanks for the book."

"I'll see you tomorrow."

Then I turned around and ran back to our house.

"I have no problem with Danny," Dad said at the kitchen table. "Should I?"

"No."

"He's never had much parenting. Elwood is some kind of stiff."

"You mean harsh?"

"He has a temper."

"It was just one of those things. Danny cleaned up Wally—"

"He did?" Dad interrupted. "Well, good for him."

"So, yeah. He cleaned him up and we were trying to get Wally to behave when Danny said he was going up to Smitty's for a burger."

"He invited you to go along?"

"Yes."

"I guess that's okay. I wish you had cleared it with me first. You could have texted."

"I did text. Maybe you were out of range."

"Okay. Still, this is all new, so let's just be fair about things."

I wore a pair of pajama bottoms and a fleece and had a cup of cocoa in front me. Dad had one too. For once he wasn't playing with a motorcycle part. Maybe he figured he needed to pay attention, because his daughter had gone out with a boy in a car. I didn't know what he was thinking. He was being so calm, though, that it made me more jittery than if he had been upset.

"We haven't had a kind of birds and bees talk," Dad

said, his face going a little bright under his beard, the cup at his lips. "You know what I mean."

"Oh, geez, Dad."

"I don't mean about the mechanics of men and women. I suppose you know most of that."

"You are *not* doing this," I said. "I'm going upstairs."

"Hold on a second," he said, and reached across the table and put his hand on mine. "I'm not going to lecture you. It's just that boys, at Danny's age, boys are just, well, they're more like wild ponies than like humans."

"Wild ponies, Dad?"

"Not ponies, maybe, but something wild and just bent on . . . procreation. On moving their gene pool further into the future."

"This is the weirdest conversation we've ever had."

"What I mean is, girls sometimes think about love, or friendship, while guys . . ."

"I get it, Dad."

"That doesn't mean a boy doesn't like you. You're just playing at slightly different games. Think of it as if you're playing gin, and he's playing, I don't know, spades or poker."

"This conversation is officially closed."

"But you're both still playing cards, is the point. I'm not just talking about Danny. I'm talking about guys in general."

"Are we finished?"

"I guess we're finished. I'm sorry if I didn't do this well."

He shrugged. He took a sip of his cocoa. I went around and hugged him.

"I know what you're trying to say," I said, pulling back and heading up the stairs. "You've done your job."

He didn't say anything. A while later I went to the top of the stairs and listened. He had the heating wand going, soldering something. I smelled it and heard it. I went back into my room and tried to read for fifth-period English class, but I felt confused and jumpy in my gut. We were reading *A Separate Peace,* all about a group of boys in a boarding school in southeastern New Hampshire. We were supposed to reach chapter seven for tomorrow, but I couldn't concentrate for thinking of Danny's sideburns, the way they framed his face when he looked at you, the way he danced with Wally, happy and sweet, both of them having a pal at last.

I couldn't fall asleep until late. I didn't even try to fall asleep, honestly, because I kept thinking of Danny, of Wally, too, and my stomach felt buttery and unsettled. I texted Holly, my one true girlfriend, about twenty times, but I didn't want to go into the whole Danny situation with her. Not in texts. Around eleven I typed I'd see her before French class, then I listened to music for a while and finished some geography homework. Usually doing homework makes me sleepy, but I sat on my bed a long time and listened to the spring peepers calling, and I thought of what I should wear the next day, what I owned to wear, and that got me up and going through my closets, and it was ridiculous to do that so late at night.

I heard Wally a couple of times too. I heard him move and heard his chain clink, and I imagined he didn't sound quite as lonely as he used to when he wasn't cleaned or fed well. Just hearing him got my stomach going more, and I finally shut off all the lights and listened to him, listened to everything, and I felt empty and quiet and filled with trembles. Later some geese went over the house, and that got me crying a little. I don't know why. They sounded so beautiful and distant, but they also sounded like they called to every human they reached, called us to something higher, something eternal, and I was almost glad when the night was quiet again.

Then, around the edges of my bed, in the small house sounds, I started thinking about Mom. She had a statue on a town square in upstate New Hampshire, up in a tiny fishing village, which was the only piece of art she ever sold. She got paid $750 and there had been pictures in the paper, and underneath her photo had been a line that read "Local Artist Places Work in Bolston." I had never been to the village, but I knew the pictures by heart, and I wondered if the statue was still there. One of the pictures captured Mom perfectly: She looked long and lean, strong, with a thick head of hair and fairly dark brows. She appeared slightly exotic, but vulnerable, too, though you wouldn't see the vulnerability unless you knew to look for it. She had a half smile on her lips, and I always thought, when I looked at the picture, that she had a joke in her head that no one else quite understood. She looked proud, too, because she had sold an art piece, put it up in her hometown, and maybe not everyone thought she was the greatest thing around, but on this day, this moment, she had accomplished something. Beside her was the abstract sculpture, made of bicycle parts, and when you looked at it, you saw it was a man throwing a fly line. She had managed to convey the sense of water around the man's legs, and although I only saw it in pictures, it looked pretty good to me. Whimsical, the newspaper said, but representational, too. People liked it and it suited the town, a quote said.

It was my mom's best day, I always imagined. One of her best, anyway.

I was still thinking of Mom, dozing almost, when I heard Danny and his father fighting. It sounded crazy and loud, and I couldn't conceive of being awake and so violent at that time of night. I had heard them plenty of times before; everyone had, but no one talked about it much.

Elwood was a bitter man, a man not to be trifled with, as people said, and their voices went careening around their house and yard and then went quiet suddenly. In the absence, I almost wondered if I had heard the argument at all. It reminded me of thunder, something you hear far away but approaching, and I held on to my stuffed dog, a Dalmatian I had named Dougie years ago, and I listened to hear them again, but everything gave way to the peepers, and finally I did too.

EIGHT

I MET HOLLY before French class. She came speeding through the hallway, her books pressed against her chest, her Uggs too thick for spring. I wondered that her feet didn't sweat off into pools of water, but I figured she liked the way they looked for some reason, so she went with them. She wore her hair differently too, pulled back and up, so that it gave her cheekbones every advantage. Although it wasn't charitable to think it, I always thought she looked a little like a crazy squirrel, stopping and starting and sitting on its tail, her hands small and fidgety. She was under five feet tall and was finished growing, and now, as she said herself, the only thing left was to get wider.

She didn't really listen, was the thing about Holly. She talked without hearing herself, or reading the person trying to take it in, but that made her funny at times. She had no filter; whatever she thought flew right out of her mouth. The squirrel metaphor worked because wherever she went she dropped an acorn of conversation, hardly listened to whatever the other person said, then went on her way.

But I loved Holly. She was my friend, my bud, and I would have done anything for her. She had a fairly solid home life. Her dad owned a Jeep dealership down in Plymouth, and they had cars the way some rich people had horses. Her mom sold plastic signs—banners and flags, anything that needed stenciling—and she always had reams rolled up in the pantry off the kitchen, waiting for delivery. They had a fully stocked refrigerator and didn't think twice about ordering out for dinner. They were the only family I knew who went on actual get-in-a-jet-and-fly-away vacations.

"Such a fashion faux pas," she said as soon as she was in range, a piece of gum snapping around back in her jaws. "I mean, I thought they looked good, but now I see they look ridiculous."

"What does?"

"My Uggs. I don't know what I was thinking."

"They look warm."

"Do you have an extra pair of flip-flops?"

"At home."

"I don't know what I was thinking."

"It doesn't matter."

"I have got to go shopping soon. I need some cute sandals for summer."

"No one's going to notice the boots."

"Yes, they will. People do. Did you hear about Julia?"

Then she was off to the races, telling me what was supposed to be a juicy piece of gossip about Julia Fields, one of the cheerleader types rumored to be pregnant. I didn't care one way or the other, but I listened because Holly liked telling the story, and she bent close to me and whispered when she got to the grimiest parts, and her breath smelled of cinnamon. Then the bell went off and we both plunged into French class, where Mrs. Baboo, not her real name, greeted us all with a big, phony *"Bonjour."*

After school Holly snagged me again. She had talked to her mom, and they were going to the mall, and did I want to come? It was Friday afternoon. The weekend was here.

"I have to get home," I said. "I'm taking care of a dog."

"A dog?" Holly asked. "What dog? This is the first I'm hearing about a dog."

"It's our next-door neighbors' dog."

"Are they away or something?"

"Yes," I said, agreeing because it was an easier route to follow with Holly. "They're away."

On the bus ride home I wondered why I didn't tell Holly about Danny. Didn't mention Danny. It wasn't as though either one of us went out with boys often, or even had a date. *If it was a date,* I reminded myself. Tied up in it was my own confusion about what I wanted. Then gradually the herky-jerky motion of the bus, all the stops to let kids off, started making me sick. I put my forehead against the window and closed my eyes. The coolness from the glass made me feel better, and in a little while my stomach settled.

Wally looked beautiful in the afternoon sun. I watched him out of my bedroom window. He didn't fuss, didn't move around or try to be anyplace he wasn't. He didn't sleep, either, but simply stared ahead, just being. Dogs are a little Zen that way, and I watched him until he stood up, circled, and sniffed at the corner of his house. He peed at the edge of his chain length. Then he heard Danny come out, his door slamming, and Wally jumped up and dangled on his chain. Danny came over and thumped Wally's ribs, but I saw he kept Wally from jumping on him. I had to duck down and watch from the edge of the window, because Danny glanced up at our house, patted Wally some more, then glanced up again.

Before I knew what I wanted to do, I knocked on the window with my knuckle and raised my finger to tell him I'd just be a minute. Danny smiled and nodded. He kept petting Wally.

"I got him some stuff," Danny said, waggling an orange plastic bag at me. "At the pet store. I got him a tag with his name on it, so if he gets lost or gets away, someone will know he belongs to me. See? It says Wally and my phone number. And a collar called a gentle leader and some biscuits and a long training lead. The lady there knew about Father Jasper. She says he knows what he's talking about."

"Wally want a biscuit?" I asked, bending close to the dog.

Wally looked good and happy, not quite as spazzy as he had been. The warm sun had heated his fur and he seemed to enjoy the decent weather. Danny already had him off his pole. He made him sit before we gave him a biscuit.

"That Father Jasper guy says you should always attach a reward to anything he does," Danny said. "Even just a simple sit."

"Did you read the whole thing?"

"Yep. It was good once you got into it. It makes sense. It's all obvious once you know about it."

"Wally could be a great dog," I said.

"Sure he could. You want to work on him awhile?"

Danny did most of the work, because Wally's strength made him a risk to knock me over. But we worked together, coaching each other and coaching Wally, too. We started with simple sit, crossing our hands in front of our waist in a slicing motion. Hand signals were important because a dog can't always hear you, or there might be a loud noise covering everything, and so we did sit about a thousand times until Wally began sitting as soon as we crossed our hands close to our belt line.

Then we made him go on our left side, and we walked in circles, stopping now and then to sit. Wally got that pretty easily, so then we did sit-stay, making him sit while we walked to the edge of the lead, waited, then called him and let him come. The first couple times he wanted to climb up Danny, but Danny was consistent and kept Wally on the ground and Wally got the knack of things readily. Despite his appearance as a kind of goofy lug, Wally seemed pretty smart to me. Father Jasper was correct: Dogs want to have some direction. Without direction they don't know how to behave, or how to get along with people, so they act every which way and get themselves into trouble. Inside of a half-hour, Wally acted more confidently, did not jump up in neediness, behaved as a companion, not a nut.

We were still working with him when Dad popped around the stockade fence.

"Hey, there are the dog trainers," he said. "Or should I say, the dog whisperers?"

"Hi, Mr. Taylor," Danny said.

Dad came over and stood, watching. I felt blood come into my face. I had to open my mouth to get enough air. I couldn't believe my dad would simply show up. It was so obvious what he was doing that it made me flush and go quiet.

"Show me what you guys have been doing," Dad said, too cheerful. "This dog looks a million times better."

"Clair gave me the book by Father Jasper," Danny said. "Written by him, I mean. He lays it all out, pretty much. It's not that hard once you start looking at the world from a dog's point of view."

"I guess not," my dad said. "So put him through his paces. I'd like to see."

Dad didn't meet my eyes. He didn't seem to want to embarrass me, but he felt he needed to be there, to check things out, or something. Maybe he simply wanted to send a message to Danny. Either way, he watched attentively while Danny put Wally through sit, sit-stay, heel. Wally performed well and Dad walked up and petted him afterward, saying, "Goodboy, goodboy, nicedog."

"Wow, that's some progress," Dad said. "Nice job, Clair Bear."

I cringed. But Danny didn't seem to notice.

"We did mostly sit stuff today," Danny said. "Tomorrow we're going to move on to down-stay and recalls. Recalls are the toughest, because once you let this dog off a leash, he will vanish."

"How do you do it?" Dad asked, squatting, still petting Wally.

"You use a long training lead. I got one today. And we'll take him over to the tennis court . . . You know, the one down in Wentworth?"

"Sure."

"Clair and I figured we might go there one of these days and work on his recall. In a tennis court, he can't run too far."

"Well, that's great."

"If you don't mind, that is. I mean, is it okay if Clair goes with me?"

My dad looked up at him. I wanted to sink into the center of the earth.

"Nice of you to ask, Danny. I think it's okay if you promise me one thing."

"What's that, Mr. Taylor?"

"You'll drive carefully. Don't say yes and don't say

no. Just think about it, okay? Kids can get a little crazy in cars."

"I understand."

"You, too, Clair. If Danny doesn't drive properly, will you give me your word that you'll get out of the car and call me?"

"Dad . . ."

"That's my one rule. Do you both promise me?"

I felt like a piece of livestock these men had decided to discuss, but I nodded. So did Danny. It was all exceedingly strange.

"Okay, Clair," Dad said, "I'm going to start dinner soon. Don't be too long, okay? Good job with the dog, you two."

He left. Weird did not begin to cover it.

Holly called me while I was setting the table to tell me about the pair of awesome sandals she bought. They were on sale, too. I held the phone between my ear and shoulder while I set out plates, folded paper napkins under the knives and forks. We left the back door open so we could get the kitchen aired out. Dad made BLTs, his favorite Friday night meal. Later, I knew, he planned to take a sunset ride with the Devil's Tongue guys and stop off and have a few beers at the Cattle Call.

"So what are you doing tonight?" Holly asked when she finished describing the sandals in painful detail. "I want to go see a movie or something. You up for anything?"

"I don't have any way to get around. Dad's going out."

"I could probably talk my big brother into carting us over to Lincoln if we pay for gas."

"I'm broke," I said, mostly because I didn't want to go to the movies with Holly and her brother. "I think I'm going to hang and watch some TV and go to bed early. I feel tired for some reason."

"My mom says it's the season change. She says whenever the season changes people get sleepy."

"Maybe that's it."

"Guess I'll see you, then. What are you doing tomorrow?"

"I'm actually helping my neighbor train his dog."

"*His* dog?"

"Danny Stewart," I said, my voice a little lower so Dad wouldn't hear it over the bacon frying. "He's got a crazy dog that lives next door and we're trying to train him."

"I don't know him. Does he go to our school?"

"No, he goes to the vo-tech."

"Grease monkey? I can get into that."

"He's just a guy."

"You're full of secrets. The mysterious Clair."

"Hardly."

"Are you dating him?"

"No. Not even close."

"Sounds to me like you are. If you train a dog together, I mean . . ."

"I've got to go, Holly. Dad wants to plate dinner."

"Okay, toodles. Or should I say, poodles?"

I groaned and hung up. Dad started taking off the
bacon. He wore his Devil's Tongue vest, its leather old and
faded from the sun. As soon as the bacon left the pan,
the noise was cut in about half. I realized it had made me
jumpy. Now that it was gone, I heard the wind outside and
the late-afternoon birds calling.

"Grab the mayo, would you?" Dad asked when he slid
our plates onto the table. He hadn't seen that I had put
out plates, so he lifted the empty ones off and set them on
the counter beside the stove.

"And a beer," he said.

"Bikers and beer."

"You know it, Harley chick."

I brought the mayonnaise and beer over to the table.
He opened the beer with his key chain.

"I like the sideburns," he said when I sat down.
"Danny, I mean. He looks like a young Johnny Cash."

"You're ridiculous, Dad."

"I'm just saying. I hadn't seen him in a while. He

looks good. I liked that he talked to me about taking you out."

"Like I'm some horrible weight one of you has to support and care for."

Dad grinned. He buttered his bread with mayo. He grinned wider.

"You sounded just like your mother then."

"The apple doesn't fall far from the tree."

"Want to say grace?"

"Nah," I said.

"Don't tell anyone I didn't give you religious instruction, then. See, I just offered it."

"Your biker group is called the Devil's Tongue, Dad. No one is going to mistake you for a religious scoutmaster."

"Amen to that."

He took a big bite. I took one too. His BLTs were always out of this world, mostly because he knew a guy who slaughtered a couple pigs every year and that's where we got our bacon. We ate for a while without talking. It was nice having the back door open, fresh air spilling inside. He drank his beer. His tattoo—he had a sailing ship on his right forearm—looked blue and yellow in the afternoon light. Whenever I saw his tattoo, I promised myself that I would have one someday. Then in the next minute I decided never to have one no matter what. I didn't know what I thought about tattoos.

"So, do you like him?" Dad asked after a while.

"Da. . . ."

"I'm not trying to pry. Honestly, I'm not. I thought maybe we could learn to talk a little more frankly or something. We don't have to be adversarial, you know. There's not some rule about it for dads and daughters."

"I know."

"So, do you?"

I picked at a piece of bacon that had fallen on my plate.

"I don't know. That's the truth. It's crazy because I've known him a long time, and now he suddenly seems halfway decent. I don't know."

"He was always a pretty nice kid from what I could tell."

"He was a jerk a lot."

"He was cocky, I remember that. Kind of a braggart."

"Sure he was. He still might be for all I know."

"He didn't have an easy childhood. Still doesn't, probably. I'd like your word that you won't go in the house with Elwood. Just stay clear of it."

"Is Elwood that bad?"

"He's pretty bad. Pretty violent. Lot of fights as a young man, lot of crazy behavior."

"Where did Danny's mom go?"

"Left. Cleared out. I don't know what happened

exactly. I'm not sure anyone does. She's probably been gone around five years or so. She tried to be a decent mom to Danny, from what I could tell sitting over here, but it wouldn't be easy in that house. Elwood breathes a lot of air. Does Danny hear from her?"

"I didn't ask him."

"I'd be curious to know. She deserved better. But I suppose it wasn't easy for him to have his mom walk away."

He realized what he was saying—how it was a quick jump to think about my mom, his wife, and how she had walked out too, but in a different way—and he flushed on his cheeks. He took another bite of his sandwich and let things settle. Then he sipped at his beer and looked out the back door.

"She was quite a pretty little thing in her day, Danny's mom. I remember her around and I remember wondering how Elwood ended up with her. A lot of people wondered that."

"What was her name?"

"She was a Jefferson girl. Her family name. Her first name was Lucy. 'Lucy in the Sky with Diamonds.' She was bright and pretty; that's why it was such a surprise to see her with Elwood. He darkened her right up. After a little while she had no light anymore, if you know what I mean. You could tell she had had it sucked right out of her, but it wasn't like Elwood got any lighter. He's a dark star."

"Sounds like you liked her."

"I did. Everyone did."

"I'll ask Danny if I get a chance."

"You seeing him again?"

"We're supposed to train Wally tomorrow."

"Oh, that's right. I forgot."

He had to get going. It was kind of cute watching him transform into big bad biker man, knowing what he was really like inside. He tied a bandanna around his head and put a fleece on under his leather coat. He checked himself in the downstairs bathroom mirror, then came out and told me he wouldn't be late.

"You take care of the dishes?" he asked.

"I'll take care of the dishes."

"Later, Clair Bear."

I kissed him on the cheek and he clumped off. A few minutes later I heard his Harley kick off, loud and throaty, its sound going off along the road a long way.

As soon as he was gone, I regretted blowing off Holly for the movies. It was Friday night and I didn't have a thing to do. I didn't even have homework, because my school was lame, for one thing, and because I usually stayed up on assignments anyway. I turned on some music in my head-phones and cleaned the dishes. It didn't take long. Then I straightened up in the kitchen, making it nice for when

Dad came home, and I was still doing that when Danny knocked on the screened door.

"Someone is here to see you," he said through the screen, because he had Wally on a leash next to him.

I don't know what it was, but that was the first time I had a funny feeling about Danny. It seemed calculated that he showed up the minute my dad had left. He knew my dad was gone. Anyone within a block or two would have known that from the sound of the Harley. As I looked through the screened door, light coming in behind him, I saw Wally and Danny as a pair suddenly, both of them needy, both of them wanting companionship, and I didn't know what I thought about that. Not about Danny, anyway.

But that thought only stayed a second. Mostly it felt good to have something to do on a Friday night. I crossed the kitchen and opened the door. Wally tried to jump on me, but Danny kept him tight on the leash, and both of them squeezed into the kitchen, like two wild things coming into a place they had only dreamed about.

NINE

ALWAYS WONDERED what this place was like inside," Danny said. "Nice. Is that your dad's stuff?"

He nodded his chin toward the motorcycle parts on the counter. They rested on a piece of newspaper. He moved over to where my dad had been sitting, and got Wally into a down-stay. Wally looked around, his big snuffle cheeks going in and out, trying to scent the bacon. A string of drool dripped off his lower lip. It was strange seeing him inside, but good, too.

"Yep," I said. "Motorcycle parts."

"I saw him go out. He's going on a ride?"

"First of the season."

"Decent. So, I figured there was no real reason to wait until tomorrow to go to the tennis court. They have lights on it. You feel like working with him now?"

Whatever I sensed before passed away, and I leaned back on the counter, trying to figure out what I felt about Danny. It was complicated. He was good with Wally; clearly, he liked the dog now that he saw what he could be as a friend. Danny appeared expectant and hopeful, that was the thing, but underneath that was a dark line that said he didn't *really* expect things to work out. A tragic note.

"I guess so," I said, answering his question. "Not late, though."

"Cool. I put a blanket on the back seat so Wally wouldn't mess things up. He's never been in a car."

"He must have been when you brought him home."

"I guess so. Then he was. But not since."

"You have the training lead?"

He nodded.

"Give me a second then," I said. "I've got to change. I'll meet you at the car."

From upstairs, I watched him cross back to his yard, Wally bounding beside him. He looked happy and so did Wally. I was happy too, I decided, but I wasn't sure I trusted it.

It was fairly cold at the tennis court, but nice, too, because whatever kids usually hung out there were gone. Someone had torn down the net from the right post in the center of the court, and someone else had repaired it with duct tape. People didn't use the court much. Kids sometimes played on the basketball court next to it, but usually they cranked around on skateboards.

Danny had Father Jasper's book with him, so when we let Wally out, we kept him close until we had a chance to read it. We sat on a picnic table and I read parts aloud. Father Jasper explained that recall, getting a dog to come to you, is probably the most important obedience skill you can teach. It could save a dog's life, he said, because if a dog took off for the road, the only thing that would save him or her was a working recall. Besides, he said, letting a dog off a leash, walking in the woods with a dog, is one of the best reasons to have a dog in the first place. It does wonders for a dog's sense of confidence and gives both the animal and the owner a necessary break and a sense of teamwork.

"You can't just make him come back, then hook him up and be done," I finished. "You have to call him to you, reward him, then let him go. If he thinks every time he comes to you that the play period is over, he won't want to come to you. It's called intermittent reward. He comes because he's not sure what the result will be. It's like gambling. That's why gambling is so addictive."

"Gambling," Danny said, patting Wally's ribs. "You a gambler, Wally boy? You a gambler?"

"If you lost every time, you wouldn't play, right? If you won every time, that would be boring too."

"Not if I made a pile of cash," Danny said. "Believe me."

"I mean in theory. It would get boring if you won every time. It's the same for a dog. The point, is you have to change it up. Let him come to you, then let him go sometimes. Other times, you can call it quits."

I felt like I was overexplaining, being prissy about getting the rules straight. Danny listened, but only out of politeness. I started to find him a little annoying. He wasn't concentrating, and his mind seemed somewhere else.

"Do you want to do this?" I asked.

"Sure, sure, sure."

"Because we don't have to. We don't have to do this right now."

"No, I want to. Sorry. I guess I was distracted. I don't know."

I snapped the training lead onto Wally. It was maybe twenty feet long, made of webbing, and the trick was to reel it in when you called the dog. No option to not obey.

He had to come at the first call, no questions. Sometimes you gave him a treat, sometimes you didn't. Sometimes you hooked him closer and did some sit-stays, sometimes you let him go away and play. He didn't know what was going to happen, but he knew it was all good, all worth investigating, and that was why he came to his owner.

Wally took off as soon as we released him in the tennis court. We closed the gate behind us.

"Give him a few minutes to sniff," I said.

"I never knew you could do this stuff with a dog," Danny said, watching Wally zoom around the chainlink walls. "It all makes sense once you slow down and think about it."

"Everything is reward or avoidance."

"He's digging this."

"Give him a minute more, then we'll call him, give him a treat, and release him."

When his time was up, we called Wally. He didn't pay any attention at all, but Danny grabbed one end of the long lead and reeled him in. Wally fought a little at first, then he ran toward us. I waved my hand across my waist. Wally ignored it. I told Danny to lift the lead and I pushed Wally's butt down. He sat, squirmy, ready to go somewhere else.

I gave him a biscuit.

"Free," I said, releasing him.

He took off.

"Do that a thousand times and we'll have him trained," Danny said.

"Pretty much."

"He's been good about learning. He's smart, don't you think?"

"Smart enough."

"Do you have your driver's license?" Danny asked as we watched him. It didn't have anything to do with what we were doing.

"Sure. Why?"

"How come you never drive anywhere?"

"I do. Dad's fussy about his truck, but he lets me take it if I need it. It eats gas, though, so that's probably why you don't see me driving around much."

"I didn't think you drove for some reason. Do you know how to drive a stick?"

"No. Dad's truck is automatic."

We called Wally to us. This time we made him walk with us around the court, doing sits and down-stays. After two laps we let him free again. Meanwhile, the night had grown colder and storm clouds wandered in from the west. The lights on the tennis court became hazy with mist. A couple kids came and started riding their skateboards on the basketball court. They set up jumps and a low rail for tricks. The sounds of the skateboards fascinated Wally. He ran to one side of the court and watched through the chainlink. He whined to go play. We used the boys as a distraction and we made him come away, sit, then release again. He went right back to watching the boys.

"I think that's about enough for one night," I said after a few more turns. "He made progress."

"He came no problem those last couple times before the boys showed up."

"You want to call him?"

He did and Wally came reluctantly. Danny hooked him to the regular lead. Wally danced around a little, but eventually he realized he needed to be serious. We walked him back to Danny's car. Danny got him in the back seat. We climbed in afterward.

"I'm going to teach you to drive a stick," Danny said. "We have to go past Shop 'n Save anyway. It's the best parking lot for learning."

"We don't have to do that now, Danny."

"I'd like to. It's not hard."

"I'll wreck your car."

"No, you won't. It's just learning the pedals. It's no big deal."

I looked at him as he started up the car. Part of me liked him. Part of me felt flattered at the attention he gave me. But then I looked over and saw those sideburns, and watched his face watch mine for signs of approval, and I wondered what was going on. I couldn't point my finger at anything, because he had been nice to me, nice to Wally, and I appreciated him for that. I admired his kindness to Wally, but when he had showed up at the screened door to our kitchen the moment after Dad left, I had glimpsed a neediness that wasn't attractive. It made me tied up to think about it.

He drove us to Shop 'n Save and slid out of the driver's seat and encouraged me to slip into it. The parking lot was nearly empty. Wally thought we were getting out when we changed seats, and for a while all I could see in the rearview mirror was his big, bony head. His tongue hung out of his mouth. I had to pull the seat up and adjust the mirrors, and Danny helped me, cheering me on, all the time talking about the feeling of a clutch and accelerator.

"You want them to meet midway," he said, using his hands as two pedals to demonstrate. "It's like riding a bike. When you first look at a bike, you think, *No way that I can sit on those skinny tires and coast down a hill.* But you do it without thinking about it once you learn. Shifting is the same way."

"I'm scared."

"Don't be. All you have to do is step on the brake to make us stop. You should push in on the clutch, too."

A small rain began. I took a deep breath. Danny talked some more. I felt jumpy. The weird thing was, it was kind of thrilling to be in the car with him, with a boy, and sitting behind the wheel of a powerful engine. I wanted to learn to drive a shift. I always had. And Danny was being nice, and I felt myself float back into a different attitude about him, a warmer one, and he was being gentle and soft-spoken. He was a good teacher. And when I tried to edge the car away from a stop the first time, and stalled, and started again, and stalled, he didn't get angry. He was patient and calm in his approach, and I realized he was a natural teacher, really. That was why he was so good with Wally and so good with me, and when I got the car going up to about twenty and shifted into second, he nodded as he if he had accomplished something and he knuckle-bumped me. It was fun, I admit it.

Plus, the car had power. It had a big, meaty-sounding engine, and we drove around in circles, my feet learning, the rain on the pavement smelling good, and Danny hopped out after a while and ran into Shop 'n Save and came out with two sodas and some Fritos. He urged me to go out of the parking lot, and I drove a couple of blocks, starting and stopping, and I did okay. Wally watched everything from the back seat and ate any Fritos we dropped.

And when Danny kissed me at the end of the night, parked in his driveway, I kissed him back. Then I kissed Wally, said good night, and ran back to my house, crazy nervous in my stomach, but happy, too, and my feet still felt the gauge of the pedals in my toes, and I was glad Dad wasn't home, glad to have the house empty, glad to have time to think.

TEN

I N A LOT of old movies, there's a scene where a girl comes back from a date and she presses herself against the door as soon as it closes, and she heaves a big sigh, happy to be alive, happy to be in love, completely transported by what had just occurred. Then sometimes she pretends to dance, holding the pretend guy in her arms, and she swirls around her bedroom or apartment, and it's all glorious and hopeful and corny as anything.

I didn't feel that way.

But I did feel good, or curious about what was going on, and I kind of liked kissing Danny. His lips had been thin and even, not wet or sloppy at all, and his shoulders had been good when I put my hands on them.

But Danny Stewart? I was kissing Danny Stewart?

I went up to my bedroom and I hurried to get into bed. I didn't want to talk about the whole situation with anyone. I used my laptop and got on Netflix, an old *Dexter* episode, and I watched and tried not to think or worry or do anything but follow the story.

Later Dad came in, his bike bouncing sound everywhere, and I listened to him toss his keys on the kitchen counter, then open the fridge. I had started to close my computer, because he might look in and I didn't want to have a late-night talk, when a text from Danny popped onto my phone. It said he'd had a nice time, did I want to go for a ride tomorrow? I wrote back maybe, then put the phone on my bedside table and pushed down in the covers.

I felt strange and tired. Just under my eyelids, I saw Wally. He ran around the tennis court and he lifted his head over and over, and it was part dream, part falling asleep, then it was all sleep. My body jerked a couple times and woke me, and once, late at night, I heard Wally the old way, out on his chain, his sighing painful and soft. Bugs were probably gnawing on him because the mosquitoes were already out, and I fell asleep thinking how one thing pushed into another and started things you couldn't predict. It was all a big domino set, sitting up and ready to be tipped over, only each junction took off in about a thousand different directions, and you couldn't know which trunk of the tree was yours. My dominoes ran next to Danny's dominoes for the time being, and Wally's dominoes ran between us, and I sensed we were heading for a new junction, but I had no idea what that would be.

Wally took to his training. It amazed me how fast he understood what he needed to learn. The weather improved week by week and we trained Wally every day after school or whenever we could grab an hour. Then one Saturday it rained right from first light and the sun never shook free of the clouds. It got cold, too, and you felt for a minute like the earth had decided to reverse itself and we were heading back to winter. I stayed in bed later than I usually do, enjoying the warmth, and when I came downstairs, Dad had the Jøtul wood stove roaring in the kitchen. He loves the Jøtul and whenever it's going he always hovers around it, making sure it's properly fed, then damped down, then fed again. He burns a lot of junk wood in it, from a guy he knows over in Piermont, a contractor who always has pine two-by-four butts and odd pieces of molding, then Dad plunks in a hunk or two of solid oak and stands back with this mighty look as if he had conquered the universe. Mom used to laugh when he did it, and called him a lumberjack, and he would say, *Building a fire is both creation and destruction,* which would get her laughing even harder.

I wasn't awake more than an hour when Danny showed up. He knocked on the back door and Dad let him inside. Danny carried a big paper bag of groceries and wore a hopeful look on his face that made me both annoyed and sorry for him. The needy side of him bothered me, I'm not sure why, and I didn't like him showing up whenever he had a notion. Besides, I was still in my pajama bottoms and a fleece, and I hadn't even glanced in a mirror.

"I thought maybe we could bake up some biscuits for Wally," he said. "They'd be a whole lot cheaper, like you said. I got brewer's yeast."

"Now that's an idea," Dad said. "Come on in and put the bag down."

I had no choice in the matter. I excused myself and went upstairs to get dressed—jeans and a hooded sweatshirt from the local university, Plymouth State, where Mom had graduated, then brushed my hair and stuck it in a clip on top of my head—and by the time I got back downstairs, Danny and Dad had the ingredients spread out on the counter. It was beyond strange. They were both into it,

I saw. Dad loved a project, but I had no idea what to make of Danny standing next to him. He had gone overboard on the groceries, and even brought a box of doughnuts from Dunkin', and it felt a little like he was buying his way into the kitchen. I don't know. For a second I regretted everything about getting involved with him, especially kissing him, then Dad started telling him all about the Jøtul stove, how many BTUs it produced, at what setting it burned best or longest, and it felt like I had landed on a different planet.

Danny didn't look at me. Not eye to eye. He kept his eyes away so that I wouldn't be able to catch them and by a look tell him to go away. He figured as long as our eyes didn't meet, he was safe to hang out in our kitchen and be part of something. It was his way of getting off his pole to find his own Daily Growler, I knew that, but it didn't make it any better.

Here was the other thing I realized: They expected me to make the biscuits. No one said anything, of course, but I could tell they thought as a girl I would have divine baking powers, powers that mere mortal men could never hope to possess, and it made me feel shaky in my hands to know how they saw me. Part of me liked the idea that I was in charge, and another part felt the sexism of it, but the rain kept falling and we were all there and the wood stove made it warm and friendly feeling. It felt *neighborly,* honestly, which was not a feeling I associated with our whippoorwill community. People didn't simply drop in and bake cookies together around that part of New Hampshire, but here we were doing it.

I washed my hands at the sink and looked out. Dad opened the Jøtul and put more wood in it. The rain churned everything brown and pockmarked, and as I turned off the water in the sink, I told Danny he should go grab Wally and bring him inside.

"In here?" Danny asked.

"Well, he's got to come in sometime. He was in here before for a few minutes, right? We can close off the door to the rest of the house, and if he has an accident, it wouldn't be the end of the world. You should walk him first, though, to see if he needs to go."

"That would be so cool if he could be in here," he said.

"You don't think he'll go crazy?" Dad asked, closing up the stove with a solid clump.

"Hard to know," I said. "Everything's new to him."

Danny headed out. I watched him through the window, not sure what my stomach was trying to say to me. Dad lifted out a strawberry-frosted doughnut and carried it to the sink and ate it in about two bites. Some of the crumbs from the doughnut lodged in his beard, and I had to make a motion to clue him in so he would whisk them out.

We both watched Danny. I'm not positive why, but it seemed like we both needed to do that. Danny let Wally off the pole and prevented him from jumping. Then he walked Wally to an abandoned lupine garden at the back of the yard and Wally did his business. Danny praised him afterward, which was advice straight from *My Pack*. Always take a dog to the same spot, and always praise him afterward. Don't play or joke around about it. Make the dog understand this is his time to do what he needs to do.

Afterward, though, he slapped his thigh and got Wally running and they splashed through the backyard toward our door. I handed my dad a dishtowel and told him to give it to Danny so he could wipe Wally down before he came inside. "Paws, too," I said.

I don't know why, but standing at the window and watching those two men do what I told them to do made the house feel more like mine than it ever had before. My mom always said a woman is at the center of everything, and for the first time I knew what she meant.

I told Danny not to let Wally off his leash when he brought him through the door. It was huge for Wally to be inside,

I could tell. He sort of trembled inside his skin, overjoyed, and his nose took in every molecule that it could. When he first came in, I went over and squatted down in front of him and petted him. I whispered in his ear that he could stay inside, could be part of our pack, if he would only mind. His eyes jerked around to see everything, his tongue out, his knotty head following his nose. He needed a while to acclimate. I made Danny put him in a down-stay and sit in the chair while I figured out the recipe.

Dad and Danny talked about cars, engines, a few people they knew in common. Dad didn't often have people over, except Jebby, and I saw that he liked it, sort of. He liked the idea of us all hanging out together, doing something wholesome, and it made me smile to think what people would say about the big bad biker guy who cooked dog biscuits with his kid and neighbor.

About a half-hour into it, when I had the first batch of biscuits mixed and ready for the oven, Danny asked if he could let Wally off the leash. All kinds of crazy scenarios went through my head, most of them involving Wally going insane around the kitchen, but he had settled down and looked pretty calm. I nodded.

"Don't make a big deal of it, though," I said. "Just reach and pet him and then simply unclip him. If we turn it into a big deal, he'll react."

"He might go after the biscuits," Dad said.

"And he might rub up against the Jøtul," I said, which was another thought I had. "But what can you do? He can't live on a pole all his life."

Danny was clever about it. He didn't let him off right away, because Wally had perked up with the sound of our voices. Besides, Wally *knew* we were discussing him. Then a little later, when I had put the first cookie sheet in the oven, Danny reached down and unclipped Wally's leash. Wally didn't move or show any sign that he knew he had been freed. Dad picked out another doughnut and carried it over to the table across from Danny. He tried to be casual, just a guy and his doughnut, but his movement made Wally's head swivel and a string of drool slip out of the side of his mouth.

"At some point," I said, deliberately keeping my voice level, "you should just get up and move around, Danny. Just don't pay any attention to him."

"He's being really good," Dad said, the doughnut going down his chute.

"He's a nice dog," I said. "A really nice dog."

"I got to hand it to you two," Dad said. "I thought that dog was unreachable."

"It was all Clair's doing," Danny said. "I never would have seen him that way if she hadn't taken an interest."

I blushed and fanned myself with a dishtowel, pretending it was the stove that made me color. Before I could say anything or do anything, someone climbed up the back steps and knocked on the door. Wally freaked, but not in a bad way. He got to his feet and let out a bark, and that bark was so loud, it made the saucepan hanging over the stove tong like a bell catching a vibration.

ELEVEN

IT WAS HOLLY.

She peeked in the window and tried to see, but the window had fogged and she couldn't seem to figure out what was going on inside. I wasn't madly in love with Danny or anything, and it wasn't completely out of the ordinary for her to stop by, but the combination of Holly and Danny and my dad and Wally made it hard to breathe.

"It's Holly," Dad said, stating the obvious.

Danny slipped the lead back on Wally as I went to the door. I pulled it open and put my eyes on her, telling her the best way I could to be cool about whatever she saw inside. She nodded, sort of, and then turned and said her

brother had brought her by, he was on his way to the hardware store for their mother, and she thought—Holly this
was, not her mom—that she would duck in and see me.

"Should I go with him?" Holly asked, her eyes busy on
mine trying to read the situation.

"No, it's fine," I said, opening the door wider.

"Good golly, it's Miss Holly," Dad said, using a phrase
he *always* used whenever Holly showed up.

"You sure?" Holly asked me. "If you're busy . . ."

I grabbed her arm and dragged her inside. With her
trailing arm she signaled to her brother to take off without
her.

"You two know each other, don't you?" I asked Holly
and Danny.

"I recognize you," Danny said. "And this is Wally."

"Hiya, Wally," Holly said, bending down to pet him.
"Where did you come from?"

"Danny's dad got him about two months ago," I said.
"We've been training him."

"Neat," she said, squatting and looking around at the
counter full of baking ingredients. "It smells awesome in
here. What are you baking?"

"Dog biscuits," Danny said.

That was the only line of conversation for a while.
Holly took off her jacket and hung it on a hook beside the
door while Danny introduced her to some of the things

Wally could do. Dad watched and resisted the temptation to eat a third doughnut. I baked and kind of liked what was going on. Since Mom died, these were by far the most human voices the house had experienced. I imagined the walls sucking in the noise, storing it for some sadder day, the old drywall trembling at the freshness of something it hardly remembered. When I looked at Dad, he smiled too, happy to have young people collecting in his kitchen. It struck me that maybe he had dreamed something like this once upon a time: family and friends and warmth and food and maybe even a good, friendly dog. Danny seemed to like it too, because he put Wally through his paces, showing him off with silent commands, and he looked kind of cute as he did it, his weirdo sideburns *très* Johnny Cash. I opened and closed the oven door and made Danny take a bite of a biscuit to test it for Wally. Everyone laughed and the rain fell hard on the roof and life seemed fairly easy when you all put your shoulders together and pushed.

If I had a pack—and Father Jasper says everyone does, for better or worse—then my pack was right in that kitchen. I could pretend my pack was bigger, or cooler, but that would be lying.

It got even better. At some point it became clear that it wasn't going to stop raining, and it became clear that Wally wasn't going to turn into a héllhound and stick his head in the oven, and it became clear that Dad wanted to go upstairs to nap but only after he captured one more doughnut. So I gave him one and he tottered away, and the biscuits kept coming out. We made a zillion and put them in a bunch of empty coffee cans Dad had down in the basement, and Holly said they would make great Christmas presents, we should remember them for that season, and that made Danny laugh so hard he had to put his head down between his knees to catch his breath.

It wasn't *that* funny, but it was, sort of, just a moment-and-place goofiness, but now, each time we pulled a sheet of biscuits, we pretended to puzzle out whom we should give this batch to for Christmas. Holly got a wounded look on her face at first, but then she saw the humor of it and we took turns nominating people for our Christmas list.

That may not sound funny, but it was. It was.

Wally was true blue the whole time, stretched out and watching everything, apparently amazed to be a part of something he had only dreamed about. This was a gigantic Daily Growler, bigger than anything he could have dreamed, and he handled it way better than I could have anticipated. After a while Holly dialed in music on an old radio my dad had next to the sink, and pretty soon she danced like a geek, her shoes off, her face red and flushed with laughing. Then a little later, when we finally finished with the biscuits and cleaned up the kitchen, we played a game of Candy Land on the table. It was the only game we had, and I sat at one end, Danny at the other, and Holly in between. The game made no sense at all, but we kept playing it. It felt like being a kid again, something maybe we all needed, and the game only broke up when Wally whined and indicated he had to go out.

"I'll take him," Danny said, jumping up and slipping into his coat. "Be right back."

"What have you been hiding?" Holly asked, her voice squeaky and wild and fitting the precise motion of the door so that her question came alive the instant Danny was out of earshot, "And why haven't you told me about him?"

"What?" I asked, standing to wipe down the counter that didn't need wiping down. "No biggie, Holly."

"'No biggie'!" she squealed. "Only that he is madly, totally, helplessly in love with you."

"Stop being ridiculous."

"He is."

She stood and grabbed me and pretended to smooch me like a boy. It was weird and I had to push her away and threaten her with a smear of the biscuit-dough sponge. She was simply being crazy on a rainy afternoon. Then she skated around in her socks, sliding back and forth on the floor. It was funny. Watching her, I had a nervous buzz in my head because part of me was thrilled that she thought

Danny liked me. Another part wanted not to get involved in some wild girl-talk speculation, and I kept rubbing at the counter every few seconds, hoping it would all go away.

Holly was being Holly. She could turn anything into fun, or at least into drama, and this was a tailor-made situation for her. She loved relationships, who was dating whom, and she kept track of things like some kids keep track of baseball statistics.

"He's cute!" she said, glancing out the window. "And when he's all serious with Wally and he looks over at you . . ."

"Cut it out, Holly."

"I'm telling you! He's going to be like the best father ever."

"Do you think his sideburns are insane?"

"I *love* his sideburns. They're the best things about him. He's so quirky."

Then we heard steps on the porch, and Holly closed her mouth and pretended to lock it. She crossed her eyes too, and that got me laughing.

"What?" Danny said when he came back in, his eyes going back and forth. "What's so funny?"

"Let's go to the movies. Or bowling or something," Holly said. "Let's go somewhere."

So we did.

TWELVE

WE DROVE PAST the movies, but we didn't see anything we wanted to watch. Besides, it was expensive and
none of us had any money to speak of, so Danny kept driving and playing us blues cuts. Holly sat in back with Wally,
and that was funny too, because when you turned around
quickly and looked at them, it seemed like they were two
people dating. I couldn't speak for Holly, but it was the
first time I had ever been with a boy in a car—except
for the ride up to Smitty's for a hamburger and then the
other night—and it felt strange and funny and interesting.
Danny took up his seat, and I took up mine, but an area
existed between us that could be claimed by either of us,

or neither of us, and yet it was somehow *ours*. We weren't a couple, no one would say that, but we weren't completely isolated from each other either. Holly stuck her head over the edge of the seat a lot, and I turned around whenever I could, but my antennae stayed fixed on Danny and noted where he moved and how and why.

"So, bowling?" Holly asked, her arm draped around Wally. "Or we could just go to the mall."

"I hate the mall," Danny said. "Pretty much, anyway."

"How could you hate the mall?" Holly asked. "I'd die without the mall. Seriously. I have mall withdrawal if I don't get there every few days."

"Have you guys ever seen the Peppermint Bridge?" Danny asked. "We could go there. Then Wally could walk around too."

"Where is it? Is it far?" I asked, not sure why it mattered.

"No, it's not that far. I can't believe you guys haven't seen it."

His posture changed now that he had a destination. I also suspected he liked feeling he could show us something we hadn't seen. He drove over toward Colton, then took a dirt road that I recognized but couldn't quite place exactly. Danny had to slow down over the ruts in the road, and twice, because it was spring, he fishtailed through a muddy patch. He liked that, I could tell, and his hands moved fast on the wheel and his feet switched rapidly on the pedals. At the same time he didn't want us to think it was a big deal. Boys had funny ways, I realized, and still I was aware of the space between us, the seat and console and sound system dials that we sort of shared.

"Keep an eye out for a sign that says 'Ellison's Camp,'" he said, ladling the car easily over a rutted section of road.

"What kind of sign?" Holly asked.

"Just a homemade sign," Danny said. "You know, the kind with a bunch of camps . . . Up here, I think."

We spun and veered off and the road got a little muddier. I would have mired it down ten times in about a quarter mile, but he kept going and finally pulled into a dirt parking lot. A hand-painted sign pointed to the right and said PEPPERMINT BRIDGE 0.7 MILES.

"What is this place?" Holly asked. "It's like some mad make-out spot. Do you bring all your girlfriends up here, Danny?"

He blushed and shook his head. I climbed out fast and let Wally jump free. He sprinted off and for a moment I thought I'd never see him again, but he simply lowered his landing gear and took care of business. Then he trotted around, his nose down, his tail up in a question mark. We stood around and watched Wally for a while. It was hard to believe how far he had come in such a short while. Before, he would have taken off, or done something crazy, but now he knew he had us to count on.

"Ready?" Danny said. "It's going to be kind of wet."

"Let me get my jacket," Holly said. "I'm not exactly dressed for hiking."

"You can make it," I told her. "Let's go."

"Ready, boy?" Danny called to Wally. "You ready to go for a hike?"

"He's never been on a hike, I'll bet," I said. "Poor thing."

"Today's his day," Danny said, and he looked right at me.

"Want me to lock it?" Holly called, pulling out of the back seat with her jacket.

Because of the rain, no one was around except us. If Wally was ever happy, he was happy that afternoon. At first he couldn't seem to believe what his brain told him was true: He got to walk through the woods off leash, smell whatever he wanted to, pee on anything he felt a need to mark, and could come back once, twice, a thousand times, for the homemade biscuits we had luckily remembered to bring. A dog doesn't want much more than that.

It was probably silly to be out hiking on such a wet day, but we had been cooped up all morning and it felt good to be outside. Wally made it more fun, because he nearly quivered with pleasure at everything he discovered. Also, it was interesting to feel the difference it made to hike with Danny. Holly flirted with him and kept trying to splash him by sneaking up and jumping into puddles near him, and he retaliated by shaking branches over her head and dumping that water on her. It felt weird, too, because they seemed to be buddy flirting, not boy-girl flirting, both of them somehow aiming it toward me. I connected them, I suppose, and Danny couldn't flirt with me unless he intended it to mean something, so he flirted with her and let it spill over. Still, Holly flirted hard, and I didn't know what that meant in the scheme of things. I concentrated on hiking and on rewarding Wally whenever he zoomed back to us through the understory.

Fog made the woods prettier. Every branch had a ghost. Everything dripped and glimmered and sagged, but you could tell the sun would pick it all up, if not the next day, then the day after that, or the one after that, and then the water and rain would be turned to strength and growth and green.

"It was some sort of mill," Danny said, looking down at the watercourse we came to after about ten minutes of walking. "At least that's what I heard. The creek is called Black Brook."

"How did you find it?" Holly asked.

"My uncle Desmond showed me. He grew up here before he moved away. He liked to go out exploring in his car. He saw everything around here."

"What kind of mill?" I asked, because it didn't quite make sense from the little I knew about local history.

"Not sure," Danny said, leading us down the hill, then straight down five cement steps. "You'll see."

It was a spillway. Someone had built a walkway underneath the drop of the creek so that you could step behind the sheet of spilling water and look out. I couldn't think of a purpose for building such a thing except as a gimmick, but Danny kept saying it was a mill of some sort and I didn't want to dispute it. I would have guessed it was a salmon ladder, or something to do with fish, but that didn't make much sense either. No matter what it was, though, it was pretty cool. We stepped to the center of the underpass and the water filled the whole world with sound. Holly started making little shrieks and yells, and her voice echoed and bounced off everything, and pretty soon we were all doing it. The water hitting the creek made a solid bassline, and our voices sounded like chirps. Wally didn't like any of it. He stayed at the edge of the underpass, uneasy about entering.

"It's okay," I said, squatting to bring him forward, but he didn't budge.

"He doesn't like it," Holly said. "Not one bit."

"But at least he's staying with us," Danny said. "At least he wants to be with us."

That was true and it was a good point.

Then for a while we didn't do anything or make ridiculous sounds. We simply stood on a rainy day in spring underneath a curtain of water and looked out. The water refracted everything and turned it hazy and wavering, so that whatever you set your eyes on wanted to be a dream. Leaves slipped off the spillway sometimes and became dots of color as they passed. It all made me feel happy inside, and scared, too, though I couldn't have said why if you had asked me a thousand times.

"Why is it called the Peppermint Bridge?" Holly asked on the way back to the car.

Danny shrugged. He looked tired suddenly.

"I mean," she continued, "why not the Tunnel Bridge, or the Underwater Bridge, or anything? Anything at all? Why Peppermint?"

"A mystery of the universe," Danny said.

"I hate when things aren't named what they should be," she said.

I ignored her and concentrated on Wally. He was gloriously muddy and happy and his tail went a million miles an hour. I thought about what Father Jasper says, how walking in the woods does a dog great good, and I knew what he meant. Wally continued to move and cover ground, but now he did it more thoughtfully, not like a spaz who felt he was going to be caught and put on a pole at any moment. He didn't mind coming back to us, because we simply rewarded him and let him continue on his way.

"I've got a little bit of a headache," Danny said when we got back to the car. "Sorry, but I'd maybe better call it a day."

"I should get home anyway," Holly said. "Clair, did you do the French homework?"

"Not yet."

"I hate that class," she said, climbing in after Wally.

"You okay?" I asked Danny over the car roof. He hadn't climbed in yet. I wondered if he had been up late, fighting with his father again.

"I don't know. Just feel a little rocky, I guess."

"Sorry."

He shrugged and ducked into the car. A minute later we were fishtailing back along the road we had taken to arrive at the Peppermint Bridge.

Danny texted me almost as soon as we got home.

You want to go for a ride on Wednesday?

I wrote back a bunch of question marks. A few seconds later he texted again.

Teacher in-service, it read. *No school.*

Maybe, I wrote back.

It struck me as a little strange that Danny knew the school schedule better than I did.

Around eight Holly called and wanted to go over everything that had happened that day. She wanted to know what I thought of Danny, did I like him, what did I think of his car, what did I think of his sideburns, wasn't he good with Wally, and on and on. Listening to her, I realized part of her truly wanted to know the answers to those questions, but another part, just as big a part, wanted to see if I had anything to say about Danny flirting with her. Or at least what he thought about her. She didn't mean it to be selfish, it was merely human nature, but she had questions inside the questions.

"Peppermint Bridge? It wasn't a mill," Jebby said. "It was rigged for a turbine. It powered a commercial dairy farm up that way. Isn't that right?"

He looked across the kitchen table at my dad. My dad nodded.

"I haven't been up to that place in a million years,"

Dad said, his hand tightening a nut down on a bolt that had something to do with an engine mount. As usual he had a bunch of things spread out on a newspaper on top of the table. "I'm surprised it's still in one piece."

"Oh, they built things to last in those days," Jebby said, swigging a jolt of his beer. "Not like now."

"We build things just as good now as we ever did," Dad said.

"Not projects like that. Not dams and things. I'll admit, planes are better and cars, for the most part, but dams and bridges? No way."

I knew they had launched an argument that could go on for hours, so I interrupted.

"Did you guys go to school with Elwood, Danny's father?"

Jebby nodded and peeled his beer label.

"He's one strange bird, I promise," Jebby said. "He liked nothing better than to get into a fight. I never saw him beaten. It wouldn't have mattered if he had been beaten. He just liked hitting and liked getting hit."

"How do you mean?" I asked.

I had an egg sandwich on a plate, but I didn't want to sit at the table with them. I stood next to the counter and kept an eye on Danny's house. He had Wally inside with him. At least I didn't see Wally outside on the pole.

"He's a bit of a socio-something," Jebby said. "A whatchamacallit?"

"A sociopath," Dad said. "Most people, they get in a fight and they stop when they've vanquished the other guy. You know what I mean. But not Elwood. He would keep kicking the guy, punching, even when it was clear he had won. People had to pull him off to get him to stop, and even then he'd try to get back to the guy on the ground. He was like a crazy person, really."

"That's some family, I'm telling you," Jebby said. "Hard people, believe me."

"Danny's nice, though," Dad said, glancing over at me.

"He's pretty nice," I agreed.

"Of course, you shape wood with a plane, you blame the plane if the work doesn't come true, not the wood," Jebby said.

"What's that supposed to mean?" Dad asked, his look going over the pair of reading glasses he wore. "You just say anything, Jebby, don't you? You live to be controversial, I swear."

"I mean, the child is the father to the man. Isn't that right, Clair? The way a child is raised is the way he ends up turning out."

"Maybe," I said.

"Sure it is," Jebby said, warming to the subject now that he had his hook in the water. "A plane shapes the wood just as a parent shapes a child. You don't blame the wood if it doesn't come out right, do you? No, of course not. You blame the plane."

"So parents are carpenters? Or block planes?"

"It's a metaphor," Jebby said, his eyes running into mine to see if I approved.

"Jebby, you're just a regular philosopher," Dad said, and went back to fiddling with his project. "It must be like a rush hour inside your head with all those thoughts driving around."

I finished my egg sandwich and ran my plate under the faucet. Then I straightened up the kitchen from earlier. I put all the ingredients for biscuits away and hung the dishtowel on the door of the fridge. The kitchen looked as tidy as it could be with my dad's engine projects scattered around and Jebby lounging with his heavy boots under the table.

"I'm going up," I said. "It was a long day."

"What are you watching these days?" Jebby asked, because we both watched a lot of movies on Netflix.

I told him and he traded back a few recommendations.

"Good night," I said when we finished.

"I should be shoving off too," Jebby said, tilting his beer back and finishing it.

I went upstairs and brushed my teeth and washed my face, then climbed into bed. The house felt cold and damp and I switched on a heating pad I sometimes used for a backache. It only took a second to start throwing heat and I felt my body spilling down, down into the bed and through the floor and into the earth. I imagined all my parts coming undone and melting away. Distantly I heard Jebby's bike start, stall, then start again. A while later I listened to Dad turning off lights and slowly making his way upstairs. He sang an ancient Steve Miller song under his breath, but the song mixed with the sounds of the house, and the wind outside, and soon the world went away and didn't come back until the morning.

THIRTEEN

I DON'T KNOW the family," Mrs. Cummings said. "The Stewarts? I can't place them."

"Elwood and Desmond," I said. "Strange names, I know. And Danny is Elwood's son."

"Danny, huh?"

She looked at me. Beside her chair she had a bucket of carrots to peel. The tips of her fingers, and her nails, already glowed orange with carrot skin. The door stood open to a nice morning.

"He's Elwood's boy," I explained.

"Elwood Stewart? Yes, I guess I know the name. Funny that I can't place him. And Desmond?"

"Jebby says Desmond used to steal porch furniture

and things from people's houses. Things outside, and he would try to pawn them over at Gary's."

"Oh, I remember that. I remember him now that you jog my memory. He was some squirrelly son of a sea cook. He was little and wiry and used to wear big black boots, and the rumor was he had a knife that fit in one of the boot tops and that's why he always wore them. That's who you're talking about?"

"Well, I only know Danny."

"You keep your wits about you. Don't cross those people. Are you sweet on Danny?"

"No, not really."

"What does that mean?"

"It means we kind of like each other, but it doesn't count for much."

"That's how it starts," Mrs. Cummings said. "That's how it always starts."

I noticed she had new earrings. Or at least earrings I hadn't seen before. They glimmered blue and a little purple like sapphires, only fake, of course.

"Where did they come from?" I asked, mostly to change the subject.

She touched her earlobes and smiled.

"My hubby gave them to me. How about that? He found them in an attic he was cleaning out, doing an odd job for a rental firm down in Concord. The earrings might actually be worth something. At first I thought they were just costume, but good-quality costume, but now as I wear them, I'm not so sure. They have heft and the settings are pretty nice."

"You should take them in to get them appraised."

"I intend to," she said, picking up a carrot and peeling it down as though she were whittling a stick of wood. "I just haven't had a minute."

First bell went off, loud and crazy. Mrs. Cummings put the heels of her hands over her ears, the carrot and the peeler sticking out like rabbit ears.

"I should go," I said, standing. "Good luck with the carrots."

"I'll let you know."

"About the carrots?"

"No, the earrings. And look out for those Stewarts, you hear?"

I nodded and hurried through the kitchen, then the cafeteria, then into the hallway, and finally into Mr. Masteller's social studies class. Mr. Masteller gave me a sideways look as I found my seat. He sat at his desk and did roll call from there.

That's how school went until Holly texted me during the last period of the day. She said:

Danny in parking lot. Wants to take us for eyes cream.

* * *

A dozen questions flitted around my head as I filled up my backpack with books at my locker.

How did Holly know Danny was in the parking lot before I did? And what does Danny want, anyway? Doesn't he have other things he should be doing? Did he text her? And when did he get her number?

Like that. A thousand questions like that.

He was smart about showing up, though. He had Wally with him. When I came out, he stood leaning on his car, Wally sniffing around the parking lot at his feet. A few girls stopped and bent down to pet Wally, and a Frisbee skidded on the pavement right beside the car and made Wally hop to one side, but Danny had his best game going and looked kind of like a rebel—all jacked-up car and sideburns—if you didn't know him any better. Holly already stood next to him, not bothering with Wally, really, but making sure to wave extra hard when she saw me. And it was *weird* that she waved so hard, because I knew it meant to convey an entire string of reassurances: *Hello, how are you, here's this guy you found first, and I'm standing here innocently beside him, and the dog you guys are training together is right here too, no, no way I'm interested in him. He's all yours.*

That's what her wave said.

*   *   *

"My treat for ice cream," Danny said when I came closer. "Let's go to Fat Bob's. What do you say?"

I knew somehow he had rehearsed that offer, because he said it casually, just throwing it off, but underneath he meant it harder.

No matter what, though, it beat riding the bus home.

"Eyes cream," Holly said, using an old joke line between us. "I'm starving."

"What do you say?" Danny asked. "Then I can swing you both home. I've got nothing to do this afternoon."

"Me neither," Holly said.

I shrugged and did something a little passive-aggressive. I grabbed Wally and hopped in the rear, and when Holly protested that she would get back there, I told her not to bother, I wanted to spend time with Wally. It made everything awkward for a second, until Danny spun his keys around on his index finger and walked around the front of the car. Holly tried to catch me with *meaningful glances*, but I suspected, also, that she didn't hate the idea of riding up front with Danny. It made my bones hurt to think it all the way through.

So we went. Danny revved the engine like a madman as he queued up for getting out of the parking lot. It was a boy thing. Other guys around the lot gunned their engines in answer and the whole thing struck me as idiotic, but inevitable. Holly sat in the front with one hand on the dashboard, the other on the seatback, and she looked like a baseball player taking a lead off first base, her weight shifting back and forth. I knew she wanted to be sure to include me in everything, because to do less was to ratify certain notions about her and Danny.

I put my head against Wally's shoulder and took a deep breath. He smelled like dog, but that was a good smell, I decided. He leaned into me a little and I hugged him hard. His tongue hung like a spool of wrapping paper from his mouth, and his teeth held small bubbles of air near his gum line.

At Fat Bob's I ordered a child-size portion of rocky road. Danny got French vanilla with sprinkles, and Holly ordered chocolate mint with a side of maraschino cherries. It wasn't exactly ice cream weather, and the girl who served us closed the slide window as soon as she took Danny's money and made change. Clouds had moved in to cover the sun, and Mount Moosilauke, the tallest peak nearby, still had a cover of snow. Still, we sat at one of the picnic tables they had out near the parking lot and ate the ice cream and watched Wally vacuum the area around the tables. His flubbery lips rattled and his nose took in breaths deep enough to inhale the scent of every dropped ice cream from a decade gone by. Now and then he stopped what he was doing and looked at us, wondering where his ice cream was. It was funny and sad and Danny finally trotted back up to the window and ordered him a plain vanilla on a sugar cone.

"He'll like that," Holly said, popping one of the cherries into her mouth.

"I wonder if it's good for him," Danny said as he came back and resumed his seat. He had nearly finished his own cone. He speared it in his mouth and then he did something that kind of went right into my heart. He pretended he was going to eat the other cone, and Wally sat, squiggle-butted, and you could see all that yearning in the dog's eyes. Danny smiled and slowly, slowly moved the cone toward his own mouth. Wally watched, a sting of drool yo-yoing down and glinting in the dull sun, and then Danny began talking real low and whispery.

"If there was a good dog, I mean a really good dog, a special, ice-cream-eating dog," he said, not letting his eyes go anywhere near Wally's, "and if that dog happened to be anywhere nearby . . . if he happened to be sitting in this ice cream place and had been really good, no-kidding good, supergood, do you two think that dog, a dog like that, well, do you think he would deserve a cone of his own?"

"Oh, you're torturing him!" Holly said, but I could see she thought it was cute too.

"And if that dog did get an ice cream cone, if he was one lucky dog, maybe the luckiest dog in the world, do you think that dog would promise to eat the ice cream like a proper gentleman? Do you think he would show good manners and not wolf it all down like a big hound dog?"

He glanced at Wally and Wally wiggled his rear end on the ground, nearly crazy with wanting that ice cream.

Then Danny looked right into Wally's eyes and he stopped fooling.

"You *are* a really good boy," Danny said. "You're a really, really good boy."

And I don't know why, but tears came into my eyes and I had to look away when he gave Wally the cone.

"He's better-looking than when you first see him, don't you think?" Holly asked on the phone almost as soon as Danny dropped me home. He had taken her home first. "I mean, he sort of grows on you."

"He's okay," I said.

"I can't figure you, Clair. Do you like him or not? I think Danny is wondering too."

"Danny can wonder all he likes."

"But do you?"

I lay flat on my bed, looking up at the ceiling. Dad would be home any minute, bringing subs from Poulchuck's Deli. I wasn't hungry. Dad loved subs from Poulchuck's, I knew, so I listened for his truck. He always made it into a big deal when he brought home subs, spreading out paper plates and extra mayonnaise and fussing with the condiments. He had to have Lay's Classic Potato Chips, too, and a large Dad's Root Beer. I tried to match his excitement on the days he brought home subs, because I knew he felt like he was doing something special for me. It was funny, really, and a little sad, but I wanted to meet him at the door when he came in from work.

"I don't know if I do, Holly," I said. "I honestly don't. He's nice. He is. I don't have anything against him, but I guess he was never the kind of boy I imagined hanging out with."

"Seriously?"

"I mean, did you hear him gunning the engine when we drove out of the parking lot? I never imagined being with a boy who did that."

"Most boys do that kind of thing, don't they?"

"I guess. But with the sideburns . . ."

"I love the sideburns!" she said, squealing a little when she said it.

She had said that before and it annoyed me.

"You take him, then," I said, feeling bitter and lousy as I said it. "You take him for a boyfriend."

"Don't be crazy, Clair. We're just friends."

I didn't say anything. I didn't want to fight with Holly. I didn't even know if I liked Danny in any special way, but I didn't appreciate her poaching, either. It tied me up to think about it all, so I was relieved when I heard Dad pull in the driveway.

"Got to hop," I said. "Dad's home."

"Okay, I'll talk to you later. You're really weird sometimes, Clair."

"I don't doubt it."

We hung up and I glanced in the mirror on my way out of my room. My hair looked like a rat's nest. I shrugged and hustled downstairs and arrived in the kitchen as Dad did. He lifted up the plastic bag from Poulchuck's and smiled a big smile.

"Best subs in the universe!" he said. "Made by Doris herself."

Doris owned Poulchuck's, and I always wondered if Dad had a crush on her.

"Sorry, I was on the phone. I'll get the table set."

"I'll wash up. Crack that Dad's Root Beer, would you?"

He disappeared in the hall bath and I heard him

splashing around. His boots made a heavy sound on the floorboards too. By the time he finished cleaning up, I had the table set with paper plates and salt and pepper and a bowl for the potato chips. I poured his Dad's Root Beer over a glass of ice and handed it to him. He raised it to me quickly because the carbonation had turned the top into a moat of blond fizz and he knew I loved that. I had been sipping off his sodas for my entire life, and I did it now and felt the bubbles sizzle in my sinuses. He smiled and winked at me, which was something he always did too, whenever we did the soda thing.

He unwrapped his turkey-Swiss-bacon, extra mayo, half hots. I had a straight tomato-mozzarella with oil and vinegar, hold the hots. It's what we always ordered. The subs looked like swords of bread stuffed with deli food.

"How was school?" he asked around his first bite. "Did you learn anything today?"

"A million things. I'm a genius now."

"Really? Then it was a day well spent. Name one thing you learned."

"Mrs. Cummings got new earrings from her husband."

"Good for old Agnes."

"You really knew her when you were younger?"

He smiled and flicked a piece of lettuce off his beard. Then he drank some root beer and chomped a few chips.

"Of course I did," he said when he had mouth space. "You know that. Is that so hard to believe?"

"I just can't picture it. I can't see it somehow."

I had a bite of my sandwich, but I still wasn't hungry. I didn't particularly want to tell him about going for ice cream with Danny, but I didn't know why. I tried another bite and had trouble swallowing it.

"Everyone was young once upon a time," he said. "That's a fact of life."

"I know, but I can't picture it."

"Well, I had an interesting day too," he said, herding a few more chips onto his plate. "We did a job over by Hanover, and I can't tell you what the house was like. You would have loved it, Clair Bear. All post and beam, like the restaurant you like over in Lincoln, and it had a fireplace that covered half the southern wall. It was right out of a magazine, I swear. The thing about it was, it wasn't fussy. It was just a place these people had, but they had plenty of money, you could tell, but mostly they liked the house for the fun it promised. I don't know. It's hard to explain."

"Did you put in a big system?"

"Oh, yeah. Top-of-the-line everything. They got the full setup, believe me. I don't know what the final bill will be, but it will be steep."

"Do you like doing what you do, Dad? Did you like putting in that system today?"

He smiled down at the sub. He didn't say anything right away. I realized I had never asked whether he liked what he did every day. I had taken his work for granted. It didn't make me proud to see that for the first time. Somehow it felt a little like ignoring Wally all those days.

"It maybe isn't what I dreamed of doing."

"You dreamed of being a racecar mechanic, right?"

"Or something. I used to think I could have been pretty good at designing new vehicle models. You know, like the new Chrysler or Ford for such and such a year. I liked doing that kind of thing as a kid."

"You never told me that before."

He kept looking down at the sub and I wondered if he felt emotional. I tried to see his face, but then he looked up and put a smile on his lips. But it wasn't a real smile, and I watched him closely, trying to fathom what he was feeling at that moment.

"Well, it wasn't anything my parents encouraged, I guess. In shop class I used to make models of clay and sometimes soap, even. The shop teacher was a guy named Mr. Gallo and he was a good sort of teacher. He took an interest and he liked cars, so we would talk about the new models. It sounds funny now, but that's what we did. He subscribed to *Popular Mechanics* and *Auto Digest*, I think, and he passed on the issues to me after he finished with them. I didn't even know there was such a job as a designer for new cars. That's how raw I was."

"Did you ever think about moving out to Detroit or something?"

"Thought about it, but I met your mom and I didn't really know how to go at it. So I did the heating business thing and that's worked out okay. A job usually outlines your life, I guess."

"But that's why you like monkeying with the Softail, right?"

"Maybe," he said. "Probably so."

"I never thought about you doing anything else."

"Most people let go of a few dreams along the way. Jebby wanted to be an astronaut. Did you know that?"

"That's just wrong," I said, laughing.

"He was sort of serious about it. He used to take off school to watch the space mission launches. Of course, if he had been serious about being an astronaut, he would have made it a point to stay in school when they had a mission launch, but he didn't know that at the time."

"Jebby—"

Someone knocked on the door. Dad raised his eyebrows, wondering. I held up my finger and went to the door and opened it just a little. Danny stood on the step with Wally beside him, his desire to come inside transparent. But I didn't open the door all the way. Instead, I blocked the opening, reached a hand down to say hello to Wally, then shook my head and told him we were in the middle of dinner.

"Oh," he said, his face folding down, "sorry. I'm sorry."

"It's okay. We're just having a family dinner."

I didn't even want to think about submarine sandwiches being a family dinner, but that's the way it was. He nodded as if understanding and he backed off the porch. I felt terrible, but I forced myself not to give in and I closed the door.

"You two okay?" Dad asked when I sat back down.

"Sure."

"You didn't want to invite him inside?"

"No. Not right now."

He nodded. Then he grabbed some more chips and took a humongous bite of the sub.

Before bed I went out to see Wally. Danny had put him on his pole. I figured his father would have some say about whether Wally came inside or not, and it wasn't a bad night to be outside, anyway. I squatted down and rubbed Wally's chest. I kept glancing behind me, half hoping Danny might appear, but I couldn't see his car in the driveway. He was probably out cruising somewhere, maybe over at Holly's for all I knew, and that line of thinking got me tangled up.

I put my forehead against Wally's forehead and neither of us moved for twenty seconds or so. The world smelled good. It smelled of rain and mud and trees taking leaf. I thought of what my dad had said at dinner, and about his idea of being a designer, and about the look on Danny's face when I didn't invite him inside, and it felt as though I had swallowed a hot coal and instead of going out it burned brighter with each breath. In Shakespeare's play *Julius Caesar,* Brutus's wife, Portia, dies from eating coals, I knew, because we had read about it in ninth grade literature. When I read it, and when Mrs. Philipone explained it, I didn't believe a word of it, but now I did. It made all the sense in the world.

Later, from my bed, I heard Danny come out and let Wally off his pole. I rolled over and ducked down by the window and I watched him. Wally tried to jump up, but Danny corrected him and lowered his own posture so Wally could give and receive affection without misbehaving. Danny rubbed him a long time. Then he leaned forward and put his head against Wally's shoulder and he was so still, so unmoving, that Wally actually sat and let him keep doing it. The sight of Danny finding some comfort in Wally made me choke up. I wanted to call to him and tell him I was sorry for not letting him inside at dinner, but once a thing was done, it was done.

Finally Danny stood and led Wally on a short loop around the yard. Danny looked over at our house a couple of times, but he didn't keep his eyes on it for long. He led Wally inside afterward and Wally trotted at his side, happy to go with him, happy to go anywhere.

FOURTEEN

ON THE TEACHER in-service day, Danny texted me first thing in the morning asking me to go for a ride, and I said yes, okay, because it was a pretty day and I had nothing else to do. Dad was out of the house early, still working on his job over by Hanover, and I left a note saying I was going for a ride, not sure when I would be back, but that I'd call.

I checked my phone for texts from Holly, wondering if Danny had invited her, too. We had been a little brown with each other at school, talking, but not really. She had mentioned doing something with her brother on the in-service day, but I couldn't remember what it was. We didn't talk much about Danny.

"Any destination in mind?" he asked that Wednesday morning when I climbed in. Wally sat in the back seat, happy and drooling. Holly wasn't there, but it was possible he intended to go pick her up.

"I'd like to go see my mom's statue."

"Where's that?"

"Bolston. It's north of here. It's a fishing village."

"How far?"

"I don't know. New Hampshire isn't that big, but it's probably pretty far."

"I've got a map in the glove compartment. Start navigating and I'll get us going."

It was that easy. He didn't mention Holly and neither did I. I was on my way to see my mom's statue. That seemed incredible.

Danny wore a pair of jeans and a red flannel shirt untucked over a blue T-shirt. He drove north according to a bubble compass on the dash. I unfolded the map and spread it on my lap, but it took me a while to find Bolston. It was way up on Route 3, the center spine of New Hampshire, up in the Pittsburg area.

"I don't even know if the statue is still there," I said after we had a rough route planned out. "They might have taken it down by now."

"Your mom did it?"

"Yes, but I don't know much about it. It's kind of like a family legend."

"I know about those."

"You never talk about your dad. Or about your mom."

"Not much to say about them."

"Anyway, we might be driving all that way for nothing."

"It's only an hour or two and it gives us someplace to go."

"As long as you feel that way."

"We need to walk Wally soon. Not sure where he's at on the bathroom continuum."

"Okay."

"Was your mom an artist?" he asked. "I mean, I know she taught art, but did she, like, do her own stuff?"

"I guess so. They paid her for the statue we're going to see. Something, anyway. It's a fishing village."

"You mean like an Indian village?"

"No. I don't know exactly. That's what they always said about it. I guess it's a place where people go to fish. Something like that. The subject of the statue is fly-fishing. But I guess she used bicycle parts, and it got a little write-up in the newspaper."

"Cool."

"It's her only professional piece."

"And you've never seen it?"

"Nope, just pictures."

"Well, that's good then. We can grab some sandwiches and we can try to find it. It will be like a treasure hunt."

We drove. Eventually the road numbers started making sense and I was able to direct him better. Danny played me a variety of blues, music that he admired, and he talked about why he valued it. I liked seeing him that way. He said the blues were sad, but hopeful, too, because as glum as the lyrics might be, as much as the songs were often about loss, the beauty of the rhythms spoke to the pleasure of transformation. Something like that.

As he talked the day grew warmer and we wound down the windows, and Wally stuck his goofy head out the back, and it felt good, it all did. I didn't mind the way I looked, and I liked how Danny treated me respectfully, and didn't think because we had kissed that we were now in some torrid sex contract. I decided that I liked Danny, although I wasn't sure if it was "like" with a capital *L* or small *l*. He was okay. And I also decided it didn't matter, that I could let it go, just ride it along and see where it took me. That maybe we would be friends, and maybe we would be more, but I didn't need to direct anything or try to shove it in any certain direction. It was a relief to come to that conclusion.

For a long time we rode north and I held Wally's head

over my shoulder, like the world's biggest, goofiest parrot, and it was pretty outside. The trees had turned green and the rivers ran full, and going north always felt like progress. I was heading to see my mother's statue, if it still existed, and that felt good too. Danny had made that possible. I had to give him that.

We walked Wally on the forty-fifth parallel, halfway from the equator to the North Pole. Danny spotted the sign along the highway, and it took us a moment to understand what it meant.

"We're halfway to the North Pole," Danny said when we backed up and looked at the sign again. It was hard to comprehend. We pulled over to a dirt turnout. Obviously, people stopped and took pictures next to the sign.

"And halfway to the equator."

"The world's big," Danny said.

Wally surged to get out. We walked him along what would be a cornfield in a couple of months but right now was only a dirt meadow filled with last year's stubble. Wally did his business and we walked over and stood against the latitude sign. Danny took pictures of me and Wally, and then handed me the phone and let me take pictures of him. Then we did some silly shots, both of us pointing to the sign and covering our mouths in surprise, joking around. He showed me the different shots on his phone, and we laughed, and I noticed that his phone seemed to be ringing a lot. He checked it each time it rang, but he never answered it.

"Who's trying to get through to you?" I asked when we got back in the car, wondering if maybe it was Holly.

"I don't know. I don't recognize the number, but I'm going to turn it off anyway."

"You have a girlfriend?"

"I don't know. Do I?" he asked.

It slowly dawned on me that he meant me, and I felt my face flush. I kept looking forward. I didn't answer and he didn't pursue it. But he also didn't turn off his phone and he kept checking it as we drove, never answering it but always pulling it out of his pocket and glancing at the number.

We hit Bolston a few minutes before noon. It was a tiny village off the main drag. One look around made me doubt the statue still existed. A sign directly over the town line said it was the PROUD HOME OF THE EASTERN BROOK TROUT. The Connecticut River ran through the town, and I realized this is what the article meant when it called it a fishing village. It was a destination for trout fishermen. Counting the number of signs about moose and deer, maybe it attracted hunters, too. The houses on either side of the main road appeared rundown and cheap. Some of them had been painted wild colors, as if old hippies lived there, and they had the usual whippoorwill yards, with beat-up cars and junked engines, broken hammocks and plastic Wiffle ball bats, leaning against trees. I couldn't see any town center, or common, where a statue might be located.

"I'm going to ask this guy about the statue," Danny said, pointing to a guy on the left-hand side of the road. The guy had his head in the mouth of an old car, his body jackknifed in to reach something.

"I don't think it's here anymore."

"You never know. Can't hurt to ask."

"I'm beginning to think it was taken down."

"Hold on one second," Danny said, and pulled the car over. "No reason to jump to conclusions."

He climbed out of the car and ran up to where the man was standing. They talked. I couldn't hear what they said, but Danny looked back the way we came, made a motion with his hand to say which side of the road, then nodded and said thanks loud enough that I heard it.

"We passed it," he said, climbing back in. "We passed the statue. It's right on the town line."

"It's still there?" I asked, my heart beating hard.

"I guess so. It's on your side. It's grown over is why we didn't see it"

We drove back the way we came, and I saw it this time without trying. Vines had covered it, looping up and obscuring it, but I knew it was my mom's work even before Danny stopped the car. It looked like my mom, strangely enough, although I didn't even know myself what that meant. It had her essence, somehow, with all the movement and bicycle parts, and vines tying it to the bushes behind it. It stood about double my height on a metal I-beam sunk into the earth. The wind tried to make the statue move, and I realized it was meant to swing like a weathervane, turning with the breeze, and some of the gears down below—down where the fisherman's belt was located— had been designed to turn. It was sort of a mobile, and sort of a weathervane, and I liked the way it looked, the way it stood, and I found myself smiling even as my eyes filled.

"There you go," Danny said. "What do you think of that?"

"It looks pretty good, doesn't it?"

"It's kind of cool. We could cut away the vines and then it would move more."

"I can't believe we found it."

"Why wouldn't we?"

"I don't know. I guess I was starting to lose hope."

"You want to clean it off?"

"Do you have any tools?"

"We could buy some clippers or something. I have a knife with a saw blade."

"Let's just use that. Maybe we can come up some other time and do a complete job on it. Now that I know it exists, I mean."

"Some people might like the vines. It makes it look pretty cool."

We tied Wally to the I-beam, and while he peed his brains out to mark his territory, we used Danny's stupid Swiss Army knife saw blade to hack away at the vines. They were honeysuckle vines, we guessed, and no one had cut them in a long time. They came away fairly easily, though, and it didn't take long to chop down the front vines. It reminded me of the Tin Man in *The Wizard of Oz*, because every time we got another vine cut away, the statue tried to move more. I imagined plenty of people in Bolston probably didn't comprehend the statue was supposed to move, if they knew about its existence at all. It felt good liberating the statue, and Danny was a champ, climbing up and nearly killing himself to get the tallest vines off. Slowly the statue began turning again, just a little, and one of the middle gears rotated too. Danny jumped down after he'd sawed the last vines free and he nearly landed on Wally. Wally skittered to one side, then he jumped up on Danny.

"It needs some oil and stuff, but it was meant to turn with the wind," Danny said, patting Wally.

"It's kind of pretty, isn't it?"

"It's very pretty. All from old bike parts."

"Mom loved junk."

"I'm sorry about her. About how things went with her," he said.

"Thanks," I said.

"It was a car accident? How long ago?"

"A little more than three years ago."

"And an accident?"

I shrugged. That had always been a question. The police said her car showed no sign of braking before it rammed into the bridge abutment out on Route 25. They said usually there would have been tire marks or some sign that she had realized what was about to happen, but they couldn't detect anything in this instance. Still, they filed it as an accident, mostly so the insurance companies would cover the loss on the vehicle at least. My father said Mom had no life insurance, so he used the car repair money to cremate her.

"Yes, an accident," I said.

"I'm sorry."

"So am I."

We didn't talk much after that. We watched the statue turning slowly in the wind. Mostly it teetered back and forth, not sure which direction to go.

*   *   *

It turns out, Wally could swim. Of course, nearly all creatures can swim, but Wally had enough Labrador retriever in him to make him crazy about water. I knew that much from looking up his breed characteristics online. As soon as we pulled into a small picnic area and let him off his leash, he flopped into the Connecticut River and took off. With the spring runoff, the water was pretty high, and I worried when he flattened out and really started swimming toward the center of the river. I figured he might keep going until the river emptied into the ocean somewhere. His ears dragged in the water. Then I remembered how strong he was, how determined he could be, and I smiled when I saw him bend in a big arc and come back toward us. He had spotted something in the water, a stick or a piece of debris, but it had drifted away before he could snag it, and so he came back.

"That's a boy," Danny said, and broke off a big piece of wood from the underbrush and threw it into the river.

Wally took off. It was impressive to see. He meant business this time, and he flew off the bank and landed with a huge splash. *This is what he was born for,* I realized, and I forgot what I had thought about his blood containing bloodhound or Great Dane. He was a Labrador retriever, at least his instinct was, and he deserved to live near water where he could swim. He was good on land,

and strong, but seeing him swim was an entirely different matter. I wondered if his paws were webbed.

"Man, he likes that," Danny said, watching him and smiling. "You hungry?"

"I am. I'll grab the sandwiches. You keep throwing for him. It will be good to tire him out for the ride home."

"He's going to smell up the car."

"That's what owning a dog is all about."

"I notice he's not getting in your car."

"Keep him exercising."

I set the sandwiches out on the picnic table. The table was in rough shape; the picnic area in general was in rough shape. Bolston looked like better times had passed it by, and I wondered about my mom spending her childhood up here, not far from Canada, a young girl in a fishing village. I knew her dad had worked in a mill, and some grandfather had been a logger, but beyond that it was all a mystery. In any event, people weren't flocking to Bolston to picnic any longer, so the town had let the area run down, and the statue had taken on vines, and that was the way it was.

We had two turkey sandwiches and a bag of sour cream and onion potato chips and two orange sodas.

"That dog can swim," Danny said, coming over and propping himself up on the tabletop once I had the sandwiches set out. "I mean, really."

"We can take him to some lakes down at home."

"We're going to have to. That dog is intense."

"Eat," I said.

His phone buzzed and he checked it and put it back in his pocket.

"What are you, like, a drug pusher?" I asked, taking a bite of my sandwich. It was good and fresh.

"Yes, absolutely."

"Somebody wants to talk to you."

He bit into his sandwich. He put the sandwich down when Wally came back, and Danny chucked the branch into the water again. Wally launched.

"Not anybody I want to talk to."

"Can we drive by the statue again before we leave?"

"Sure. We can take more pictures."

"I still can't believe it's there. Thanks for bringing me, Danny. It means a lot to see it."

"Why didn't your dad ever bring you up?"

"I don't know. It's kind of weird that he didn't. He's all tied up about my mom's death."

"How come?"

"They had a fight, I guess, right before she died. You know. She stormed out of the house and he didn't go after her, and then she drove off, and next thing you know, she's in an accident. Dad doesn't talk about it. No one talks about it. So to come up here and look at the statue, that would mean we had to talk about it. That won't float with Dad. He'd rather keep it like a deep, sad secret."

Danny took a big bite of sandwich, then threw the stick for Wally again. Wally looked a little tired, but he still went after it.

"Sorry," he said. "About your mom."

"Things happen."

He nodded.

"What about your mom?" I asked, picking at a chip. "She took off? That's what my dad said."

"She went into a state hospital down in Mass. Mental problems."

He put his finger to his temple and swirled it around to indicate she was screwy.

"Is she still alive?"

"Yeah, she lives down in Florida now with her older sister. She's not . . . what's the word? Mentally competent. Her sister is her caretaker. Legal, I mean. I'm supposed to go down to see her one of these days, but it's a long way to go and her sister is a little worried that me showing up might . . . I don't know. Unhinge her, I guess."

"That's really too bad."

"Well, living with my father wasn't any joyride for her. He can be rough to be around."

Then he changed subjects. I had more questions, but I didn't want to beat it into the ground.

"We should give him something to eat," Danny said, watching Wally.

"We have some of those pig's ears that he liked."

"So your mom grew up here?"

"I guess so."

"This is north country. Halfway to the North Pole."

"Yes, it is."

"Probably be boring to be a kid here unless you were way into the outdoors."

"Might be why she got into the whole junk as art thing. She probably couldn't afford much more. Not real materials, I mean."

"That statue is pretty good, though."

"It *is* pretty good. I'm glad it isn't horrible."

"I think it is really cool, actually. I mean, she did it to signal what the town was all about. You know, fishermen."

"I wonder who sponsored it."

"Probably an arts council or something. Some government money."

Danny took another bite, then hopped off the picnic table and grabbed a pig's ear from the car. When Wally came back, he offered it to Wally, but Wally put the stick down at his feet and waited. Food or play. Danny bent down and picked up the stick and threw it again. He didn't throw it as far. Wally didn't jump into the water this time, but simply waded in.

"He's going to sleep well tonight," Danny said.

"I heard him last night. The mosquitoes were getting him. I was glad you brought him inside."

"I was going to talk to you about that. You have any way to bring him in at your house? It's not quite working out over at my place."

"I don't know. I can talk to Dad about it. He might let me have him in if Wally is well behaved," I said.

"He's still pretty nutty."

"He's getting better, though."

"You know what I'd like to do? I'd like to bring him to Father Jasper. I'd like him to meet Wally. I'd like to show him off."

"It's amazing how fast they can learn."

"I feel guilty about leaving him on a chain all that time," Danny said.

"You didn't know any better. Neither did I."

"Yeah, but that was lousy. It wasn't fair. Once you know what a nice guy he can be, it feels even worse."

A car pulled into the picnic area. It was a man with a small dog, a terrier of some sort, and the dog started barking like crazy when it saw Wally. Danny hurried off to grab Wally, and you saw the reason for training a dog with recall. Wally didn't come, of course. He trotted over with the stick to investigate the small dog, and it was only luck and fatigue that let Danny snag him. Danny hooked him up and the man with the small dog said something about Wally and patted him.

Danny walked back with Wally in a heel. Halfway across the picnic area his phone buzzed again. Danny stopped to look at it, shook his head, and then stuck the phone back in his pocket.

FIFTEEN

FTER LUNCH we started to leave Bolston, but when we got a little south of the town line, Danny spotted a bowling alley on the right-hand side of Route 3. It was an old alley, you could tell, with a vintage neon sign blinking in the afternoon sun, an arrow pointing toward the doors. ECHO LANES, the sign said, OP-N. Next to the sign a LABATT BLUE sign blinked, and next to that a sign said BILLIARDS. Danny slowed and he twisted a little toward me, lifting his eyebrows to ask if I was interested, and I nodded and he pulled in and jammed the car into a giant pothole. His face went white with the impact, and he slowed way down, so slow in fact that it seemed the bump hadn't shocked the car but shocked him instead. He parked near a few other cars and a small Blue Bird school bus, and as soon as he turned off the engine, he hopped out and went down on the ground to look at the car's chassis.

"I hate freaking potholes," he said, his voice genuinely angry, his head poking way under. "Hate them."

"Is it okay?"

I squatted down beside him, but I didn't know much about cars or the undercarriages of cars. He alligatored out after punching the muffler with the side of his fist to make sure it hadn't come loose.

"It looks okay," he said. "I hate that. I hate when no one puts up a sign. You could lose an oil pan just like that."

He stood and dusted himself off. He took a deep breath, then reached in and petted Wally. Wally looked good and sleepy after all the swimming and exercise. Danny snapped down the locks on the doors and made sure to leave two cracked windows for Wally. He wasn't going to freeze or fry in the car, given the weather. Besides, the day had grown tired and the bowling alley had already sent a shadow halfway across the parking lot. He was more comfortable here than he was on the pole beside his doghouse, that was for sure.

"Sometimes I wish I could just keep driving," Danny said, looking up at the sky. "Sometimes I really do. And if you wanted to come along, that would be even better."

"Where would you go?"

He shrugged.

"I'd just keep going. I don't know. There's something about driving that opens me up. I noticed you didn't ask where *we* would go."

I blushed a little at that. I don't know why.

"You okay?" I asked him, because he looked a little tied up.

"I'm fine. You ready to bowl?"

"I'm a horrible bowler," I said as we walked toward the front doors. "Really bad. Fair warning."

"I'm worse. I really, really suck at bowling."

But at the same time he grabbed my hand and started running. I couldn't do anything but run with him, and it felt good to be beside him. We had had a great day and now we would have some more fun, and then we had the long ride home listening to the blues and watching the white lines come at us. I didn't know if we were boyfriend and girlfriend, didn't even know if that was something I wanted, but I knew I liked running hand in hand with him. He was still ridiculously Danny Stewart, still the weirdo with snow-shovel-shaped sideburns, but he tried to learn and be nice and that counted for something. He wasn't the dream boy you sometimes hoped for; he was the boy next door, the annoying one, the one you had known forever, but he was real and living and he liked me. That counted for something, I knew now, and I ran with him and stopped just shy of the door. When he pushed through, he twirled me around a little, being fancy, and I nearly fell against an old El Camino that someone had parked inside the lanes as an advertising gimmick. Then he twirled me again and this time it worked and I spun around, feeling surprisingly dainty, and he pulled me toward him, bent one of my arms behind my back, and stopped with his face inches away from mine.

I thought he was going to kiss me. I *wanted* him to kiss me, I think, but for a five count, both of us breathing hard, we stood and stared into each other's eyes. And I had never done that. Not once, not with a boy, not with anyone, and his eyes made my collarbones tingle and I felt my head lean back a little, inviting him, but he simply spun me back the other way and then ran past me to the shoe desk.

I walked after him, my body feeling clouded and untethered to my head, and I stood beside him and gave the clerk my shoe size, the crash of bowling balls like the sound of something violent and far away.

"Wally," Danny wrote on the overhead-projected score-card.

Beside it he wrote: "Mrs. Clair Masteller."

The last name was the name of my social studies teacher. The name of the biggest idiot teacher in the school.

He was Wally. I was Mrs. Clair Masteller.

The thing about bowling, at least for a girl, is that it makes you herky-jerky and unattractive. That's how I felt, anyway. Maybe the pink-spotted ball I selected weighed too much, but I had trouble even getting it down the lane, and Danny tried coming over and showing me how to do it. I *hated* that. His lame instruction only made me more nervous, but finally, in about the fifth frame, I bowled a nine and just missed the spare, and Danny told me "Waytogowaytogowaytogo."

He wasn't much better. For one thing, his phone kept ringing, and he finally turned it off and tucked it into his jacket, and then he bowled a little better. He clowned around a lot, throwing one ball between his legs, and another with his foot, and I knew he wanted to show off and I pretended to find it sidesplitting. It wasn't, though, it wasn't really funny, and I had another moment of seeing Danny as a somewhat desperate kid, a lonely kid who didn't quite know how to interact with the world around him, and that observation got caught up in my memory of him holding me close at the bowling alley door and nearly kissing me. I thought of what my dad said, that boys are just wild ponies at this age, and I wondered if he wasn't correct after all. I wondered, too, how it was possible to feel so many divided emotions about someone, to be so unsure, and I wished, for a minute, that my mom was around, was sitting someplace beside a fire, ready to let me come over and have hot chocolate with her and talk and talk and talk. You couldn't let some questions just roam around the world. You had to know they had somewhere to go, someplace where they might get honest attention and an attempt at an answer, and I didn't know if all moms tried to do that, but I hoped they did; I hoped moms helped their daughters understand these wild ponies, because I didn't understand them at all.

I didn't break a hundred and Danny just barely did. We bowled a second game, but the fun had gone out of it, sort of. I couldn't tell what Danny thought, but for me it seemed like we had gone halfway out on a bridge, maybe a shaky log someone had put over a creek, and we weren't certain whether it was safer to go forward or back. Danny didn't monkey around as much the second game and I bowled a little better, but near the last frame, when I walked past the Formica scoring table, he pulled me onto his lap. We had been building up to that all day, and when he finally had me next to him, his breath scented with cinnamon gum, he kissed me again. It felt clumsy and awkward, and I wanted to get up and get away from him, but his arms went around me and then something melted in me and I gave in a little. I kissed him back, my body filling with syrup, my head containing a panicked baby bird flapping around inside my skull, and for a long time we kissed and kissed and kissed. His tongue flicked into my mouth, and I wasn't sure if that was something I wanted, or understood, but then it started to feel natural and exciting and real. He slipped his hands over my hips, pulling me closer, and when he let go I stood up and pretended it was my turn to bowl, I had to get to it, all official, the game must go on, but my head rattled around and I threw a gutter ball before realizing I had jumped Danny's turn and bowled in his half of the frame.

When I turned back from my second ball, I was afraid to meet his eyes. Not afraid, that's wrong. I just couldn't meet his eyes.

"I could go for some fries," Danny said after we handed our shoes back and the clerk sprayed them down with fungal spray. "You hungry?"

"A little."

"Let's go to the bar. I can smell something cooking."

"Only if I can pay," I said. "You've paid for everything so far."

"Okay, twist my arm."

The bar was called the Oak Room Tavern, and it was a room that might lie down and take a nap when no one was around. It was 77 percent cheesy and 23 percent retro-cool, and Danny thought it was the best place he had ever seen. It was dark, for one thing, and a bunch of senior citizens played darts at the end of the bar, all of them drinking long-necked beers and talking. They looked up when we came in, but then someone did something pretty good on the dartboard, evidently, and they whooped and let us alone. A short, broad woman with a cheek stud took our order at the bar. She introduced herself as Ally, and volunteered that the fries were real, not frozen junk, and then she gave us two sodas and we carried them to a table on the side of the bar away from the dart players.

"This place is awesome," Danny said, sitting and looking around. "Do you like it? I love places like this."

"It's nice. It's nicer than I thought it would be."

"Nice? I'd like to live next to a bar like this someday. You know, like a place you could go to every day, and people would know your name, and you could just, I don't know, hang out."

"It might not be my first choice," I said, sipping the soda.

When Danny spotted a jukebox over by the restroom

door, he asked me for all my change so that he could play some records. I gave him what I had and he dug in his pockets for more, and something about the way he hoisted himself up off the chair to get to his pockets, and about the way he went over and leaned on the jukebox, made me wonder if he wasn't a time traveler. He seemed out of his time period; he was like a 1950s teenager, a boy obsessed with his car and the blues and sideburns. I couldn't tell if he came by it authentically, or if it was a kind of costume he had found to wear for the world, but it made me unsure of what to make of him. I liked kissing him, it was true, and I liked him pulling me onto his lap, the feeling of his *boyness,* if that was a word, but he was peculiar, too, and unpredictable. It struck me that you could never know another person all the way through, not him, not my mom, not anyone. That wasn't bad necessarily, just a fact of life, like wearing socks in the winter, or putting on bug spray in summer.

When the music came on, he asked me to dance with him. There *was* a little dance floor near the jukebox, so it wasn't as crazy as it might have seemed, but to dance, really dance, in the middle of the afternoon in a bowling alley didn't fit into anything I knew. But it seemed important to him, so I gave him my hand and he led me into a swing dance with him, twirling around, holding hands and gliding past him, and I saw he knew what he was doing. Ally the bartender came by carrying the fries, and she smiled at us, no problem, and after she put the food on our table she danced a little beside us, goofing around, shaking her hips, then dance-walking her way back to the bar. That spurred Danny on and he danced me harder, guiding me to try a slide between his legs, and if I hadn't seen it on an ice-skating show, I wouldn't have known what he wanted. But we pulled it off, me stabbing between his legs, him lifting and spinning, and I nearly fell but he got me back onto my feet and we lurched to the table, laughing hard and feeling absurd, but liking it too.

"We're pretty good," Danny said, laughing. "We're really not bad."

He held out my chair for me and that broke my heart a little bit.

I didn't know the happiest Danny had ever been in his life, but that moment—that moment in the bar, his face flushed, his skin glowing, his mouth cracked in a wide smile—had to be a top-ten moment for him. It was for me, too, and as I grabbed a fry and popped it in my mouth, I wondered if this was what men and women did together, this crazy sine wave of emotions, this attraction and repulsion all at once. How did people live like this? I wondered.

How did people have the slightest clue what they wanted from another human being? It seemed insane and wonderful and just about the stupidest thing on earth.

I ate fries and drank my soda, and when Danny asked to dance again, I said okay, sure, let's go.

He kissed me again on the way out to the car. He kissed me up against the wall of the bowling alley, right where people came out to smoke, and I smelled cigarettes and spring mud and Danny's cinnamon gum. We kissed better now, more comfortably, but I still wondered where you put your hands, how much you tilted your head, what sounds, if any, you were supposed to make. The analytical part of my mind kept taking little snapshots. *So this is what it means to kiss a boy, and this is how they do it, and this is where his arms go, and this is how he breathes through his nose.* I wanted to remember everything. I liked that I was being kissed for the first time in my mom's town, in her childhood land, anyway, and I liked that it was spring, just at twilight, and that the birds called to claim their territory for the night. My arm felt tired and heavy from bowling, and my lips tasted greasy from the fries, I was sure, but for a second, just a second, I let myself fall into Danny. I used him a little, because I had always wanted to fall into a boy, surrender like they did in books and movies, and it might have been any boy at that moment, but Danny was there and so he was the guy.

And I also thought: *Danny Stewart is my first kiss. He is my first kisser. His lips are the lips that I kissed first.* I had no idea if that was a good thing or not.

He took my hand when we walked to the car and he held open my door. Wally didn't even budge, he was so tired from the swimming. The car smelled like wet dog, but that was okay, and Danny kissed my neck, right near the collarbone when I slid in on the passenger side, and I reached across and popped his door lock so that he could just come in and not fuss with his keys.

"You're a gentleman," I said when he put the key in the ignition. "I appreciate that."

He shrugged and smiled. Then he started the engine and shifted into first, but his hand came over and grabbed mine, let it go to shift, grabbed it again, then let it go. I looked out the window and felt close to crying, close to laughing, close to a thousand things. I thought of my mom's statue, the way the wind made it move in tiny pulses, the gears of the old bicycles clicking it awake and asking it to move.

SIXTEEN

FATHER JASPER SAYS every time a dog is euthanized because it misbehaves, it is a mark against humanity.

Father Jasper says female dogs are better for a first-time dog owner, because female dogs tend to be more docile. Not always. But usually.

I thought of Father Jasper when the state trooper pulled up behind us.

I saw the car in the side-view mirror. In an instant about a dozen things occurred at once. I glanced at Danny and he glanced at me, and then his eyes flashed up to the rearview mirror. His body coiled; his hand reached for the gearshift and he pumped the clutch, and the engine that had been running smoothly all day suddenly burst into a loud roar and we took off. His phone buzzed again and again. I had been half asleep, half reclining against the window, but in a heartbeat that was over. I saw the lights shimmer on in the cop car, and a siren started, a squawk at least, and Wally turned on the back seat and looked at whatever was behind us.

"Danny?" I said, because I couldn't put it all together.

We hit sixty in no time. Then the speedometer really began to climb, and I knew we were going too fast. Gravel pinged against the bottom of the car, and the blues, Muddy Waters, kicked out a driving, traveling beat, and it felt like we were in a movie, only not. This was real, dead real, and Danny kept moving his eyes from mirror to mirror, his hands expert on the gearshift and steering wheel.

We hit seventy-eight miles an hour going around a turn. The back fishtailed a little, but then it straightened. Danny chewed his gum like a maniac. Wally sloshed around in the back seat, suddenly agitated and picking up on the new speed, his ears cocked high, trying to sort things out.

"Stop it, Danny!" I yelled.

Because the road was twisty. The road wasn't going to let us stay on it, and I thought of my mother, and of the way she went off the road into a bridge abutment, and everything compacted and seized in me all at once. We could not travel at the speeds we were going and hope to make it much farther, but maybe that was what he wanted. As I thought it, he geared down and he ran the next stretch at close to a normal speed, but the cop car ran right on our bumper and I saw the Smokey Bear hat on the cop, and the lights flashed and flickered and made everything impatient.

"Danny?" I asked. I couldn't control my voice.

A second cop car appeared in front of us. The cop had parked his vehicle perpendicular in a roadblock, and my mind scrambled. *This is not happening,* I thought, because the day had been fine, the day had been peaceful, and we had a couple dozen photos of the statue, and Wally had been great, and we had danced and kissed, and now a cop leaned against his car with a shotgun pointed at us. Another cop car tried to keep us pinned from behind, and Danny didn't seem to question what was going on. That was the strangest thing of all, so I turned around and looked, and Wally barked, and then Danny, somehow, reversed past the cop car behind us, rolled the steering wheel like a bumper car, and he shot off across a cornfield.

It was not the same cornfield we had walked in earlier when we stopped to take a photo at the forty-five-degree latitude sign, but it possessed the same stubble, the same ruts in the dirt, and I heard the car straining to gain traction, and I heard the cornstalks banging against the under-carriage, and not a bit of it made sense. The tires couldn't grab and the car was not made for this kind of travel, and then Danny stopped and jumped out of the car and began running.

He left the door open. Wally sprinted after him.

I couldn't have stopped Wally if I wanted to, if I had *known* what was going on. Wally thought it was a big game, and I watched as he bounded after Danny and kind of ticked Danny's foot and Danny took a header into the dirt. Two cops ran after Danny, one fat and waddling, the other skinny and young, and the young one caught him, kept his gun on him. A third cop—I hadn't seen the third one arrive, but he crept across the last fifty yards of cornfield with his gun raised at shoulder height—and shouted, *"Get out of the car. Get out of the car. Get on the ground."*

It took a long time, relative to everything that had happened, to realize the cop meant me. That I was in the car. That I had to get out. And that a cop I had never met had a gun pointed at me and he seemed ready to use it.

"Getoutandgetontheground, getoutandgetontheground, keep your hands up, getoutandkeepyourhandsontheground."

Over and over. And I still didn't get that he meant me. I looked at him and he looked at me, and I saw he was young, not much older than I was, and his left hand held the wrist of his gun hand and the whole thing wobbled. He was scared. I saw that as plainly as I saw anything, but then Wally came bounding back, not sure what was going on, and I glimpsed that Danny was spread-eagle on the dirt, two cops sitting on him.

I held up my hands like they do in television, and I opened the car door with one hand, then lifted it again. I moved my hands fast, so that he could see I didn't have a pistol or any kind of weapon. Then I fell forward, crawling out, and the cop ran toward me. I saw his feet kicking up dirt as he ran, and it was all crazy, all nutty. Wally dodged the cop and ran to me, thinking we were playing somehow, and the cop covering me ran forward and stopped directly next to my head.

"Do not move!" he enunciated.

DO, space, NOT, space, MOVE.

He had the gun pointing down at the ground, ready to use if he needed it. Veins stuck out along his neck, on his head, everywhere.

"It's the Stewart kid," one of the cops on top of Danny yelled. "Confirmed."

"Put your hands behind your back," the cop above me said.

I did as I was told.

"What's this all about?" I asked. "Are you doing this because of the vines?"

"Keep your hands where I can see them."

He knelt in the center of my back. Hard. He deliberately put his full weight on me, and I felt my face go into the dirt. I tasted dirt on my lips and tongue. He buckled a plastic cuff around my wrist.

"You have the right to remain silent," the cop on my back said. "You have the right to be represented by an attorney."

"What is this about?" I asked, my voice broken and shaky.

He kept talking, giving me my rights. I turned my head enough to see the two cops lifting Danny and bum-rushing him across the cornfield. They weren't happy. Danny's feet hardly touched the ground, and when they did, he stumbled. The cops seemed ticked off about that, too. They shook him between them. You could tell they wanted to grind him down, but the law prevented them from being as abusive as they wanted to be.

Another cop showed up as the first one finished reciting my rights. They both helped me to my feet. Then they pushed me against Danny's car. They patted me down.

"You people are freaking crazy," I said to them.

"What's your name, miss?" the cop who had held the gun on me said. The gun was gone. I was glad about that.

"Clair Taylor."

"You spent the day with Danny Stewart?"

"Yes."

"We are going to take you up to the patrol car and put you inside. Is that your dog, ma'am?"

"Yes."

"Is he friendly?"

"Yes."

"We'll call animal control for him. Right now we're going to have to let him be."

"He'll get lost. He'll come to me if you let me call him."

"Ma'am, I don't think that dog is your biggest concern right now."

"Where are you taking Danny?"

"We could leash him," the second cop said. "Will he come over if we call him?"

"It depends."

"Here, boy," the cop said.

Wally looked at him, considered, then kept on sniffing, his legs shooting him forward into the brushwood along the edge of the river.

"We'll let someone know he's here," the one who had put his knee in my back said.

"He'll get lost," I repeated. I said the words slowly so they would sink into these two dimwits.

"Can't help it right now."

They dragged me off the same way the other two cops had dragged off Danny. It was surreal; my toes only brushed the ground. We followed the car tracks back up to the road. Another police car had arrived and I caught a glimpse of Danny sitting in the back of the first car, his hands obviously behind his back. He had his head down. I tried to catch his eye, but they moved me along fast, and before I knew it I was in the back of the other cop car. It smelled of puke.

"Is this all about the statue?" I asked, because I couldn't think of anything else.

"We're taking you to the station now," the driver said. He was a big guy with a nearly shaved head. I wondered why it was cops who always wanted to shave their heads. If I were the chief of police in any town, the first order I would give would be that all the cops had to have average hair length, not this skinhead crud that this guy wore.

We drove off. The last thing I glimpsed in the field was Wally sniffing along the edge of the river. He ran like a dog free at last with nobody to bother him and not a thing to do but whatever came into his head.

SEVENTEEN

SOMETIMES LIFE is like a television show. Sometimes you find yourself living through something, and you realize that the people doing the things to you are acting out a script *they* have seen on TV, and so are *you*, but neither one of you can say anything to stop it and you both go along in a crazy sort of dance.

That's what it felt like in the back of the car. That's what it felt like when we arrived at the station in minutes, and more cars whizzed past us, and a bunch of cops closed around us and nearly lifted me from the car.

They don't have enough to do, I thought.

It was overkill. The cops liked parading around and

having something big and important to do, only it wasn't big and important, *I* wasn't big and important, and Danny was definitely small potatoes. But as they moved me inside, a female cop suddenly appearing at my side, I thought of Danny's eyes, his flashing look back and forth to the mirrors, and I recalled how quickly he had begun to drive hard. He understood something the cops understood, but that didn't add up, and I kept asking, as they pulled me along a small corridor, why they were doing this, what had we done, what was going on.

We went into some sort of holding room, decorated exactly as it would be on a TV show, with a small table and a couple of metal chairs, and little else. The female cop patted me down again, but she didn't try to be friendly, or share girl power, or anything like that. When she finished patting me down, she made me sit and she walked out and they locked the door. I started to cry, but it was a strangled kind of crying, filled with frustration and annoyance, and it ticked me off that they couldn't simply tell me what was going on.

After a while, maybe a half-hour, a new officer came in and the woman police officer came with him. She leaned against the wall. The new officer brought a pitcher of ice water and he poured me out a glass. Then he nodded at the woman officer and she went behind me and cut my hands free. I rubbed my wrists—just as they do on TV shows—and I reached forward and drank a glass of water. I drank two. The cop motioned that he was willing to pour me another, but I shook my head.

The male officer smiled. He was older than anyone else I had met there, and he had short gray hair and a clean-shaven face, and he looked to be in good shape. He had gray-blue eyes and deep crow's-feet around both eyes, so that when he smiled, he reminded me of a cowboy. I could tell he was trying to be calm, deliberately so, in order to defuse the entire situation. It was time for the talk, the TV show leveling between characters, and I sat and watched and knew how it had to start.

"So, you're Clair Taylor? Is that your name?"

I nodded.

"I'm Sheriff Hazleton. Have you been given your rights, Clair? Do you mind if I call you Clair?"

"I don't mind."

"Have you been given your rights?"

"I think I'm too young for that."

He looked surprised. He smiled. His cowboy eyes crinkled.

"You can always be apprised of your rights, Clair. But you are officially a minor, it's true, because you are under eighteen, aren't you?"

I nodded.

"We have Danny next door. He seems very concerned that you not get involved in this."

"In what? Would somebody tell me what's going on?"

"You don't know?"

"We took the vines off the statue. Is that what you're talking about?"

The cowboy officer glanced at the woman officer. She didn't say anything.

"What vines?" he asked.

"My mother has a statue here and it was covered with vines. Danny and I took the vines down."

Now *he* looked puzzled. He adjusted himself in the seat, uncrossing his legs and leaning forward a little.

"What statue would that be?" he asked, examining me closely.

"It's a statue of a fly-fisherman. It's on the Bolston town line."

"The bicycle statue," the woman officer said to the cowboy. "The one with bicycle parts."

"Ohhhhh," the cowboy officer said, nodding, finally putting it together. "Your mom made that?"

"Yes."

"And it was covered with vines and you and Danny cut away the vines? Now I get it. Sorry. I was confused."

"Isn't that why you chased us?" I asked, and I realized,

saying it aloud, that it didn't make sense as an explanation.

"No, is that what you thought?"

I nodded.

"We chased you because Danny's father was badly hurt. Did you know that?"

"What? No, I didn't know that."

"Danny's dad. Elwood Stewart. He's in the hospital."

"I don't know what you're talking about."

"His skull is fractured. Badly fractured, actually. Someone hit him with a heavy object."

I stared at the cowboy officer. Then I looked over at the female officer. They both watched me closely.

"I don't understand."

"You don't understand which part?"

"I don't understand any of it."

"Elwood Stewart—you know Elwood Stewart, don't you?"

"He's my neighbor."

"And Danny's father?"

I nodded. They went at things so slowly, it drove me crazy.

"Someone tried to kill him," the cowboy cop said. "Looks like he was in a fight and someone hit him with a car battery. We're fairly certain it was Danny."

"You're making this up."

"Did you know about it?"

"Know about what?"

"That Danny had crashed a car battery into his father's head?"

"Know about it?" I repeated dumbly.

"Did he inform you that Elwood, his father, was injured?"

The cop enunciated carefully. Cops seemed to enunciate a lot.

I shook my head.

"The battery was nearby on the kitchen counter," the female officer said. "And someone brought it down on the father's head. It looked like they had a heck of a fight, but I'm guessing most of that was the father's blood. From the looks of it, the father didn't manage to bruise Danny much."

"I don't know what you're talking about. Danny wouldn't kill anyone or even try to."

"I asked if Danny told you about the fight. He left his dad in pretty rough shape. If you knew about it and didn't report it, you could be in a lot of trouble, Clair. You could be an accessory to a crime."

"I don't know anything about it."

I turned and threw up on the floor then. Just like that. No warning, no preparation. The cowboy cop pushed onto his feet and hopped away. He glanced at the female officer. She went out to get cleaning materials, I guessed. I threw up again.

* * *

"Feel better?" the cowboy cop asked after the female cop cleaned things up. I couldn't help thinking it was typical that a woman had to clean things up while a man stood by. But maybe it was a question of rank.

"I guess."

"Danny says you didn't know anything about it. Is that true?"

"How do you know what Danny said?"

"Two officers are interrogating him. I just talked to them while we cleaned up in here."

"I don't know what any of this is about."

"Sure you do. You know Danny, right? And you know his dad. Sometime last night it seems Danny and his father got in a fight. You didn't hear anything over at your house? You live next to him, don't you?"

"Yes, I live next to him, but I didn't hear anything."

"Do you ever hear them fight?"

I shrugged.

"Do you?" he asked again.

"Sometimes. But that doesn't mean Danny did it."

"No, but if I don't miss my guess, he'll be confessing soon. That's the catchy thing. It's a hard thing to carry around an action like that. To not tell anyone, not even his girl."

"I want to talk to my dad. And I'm not his girl."

188

"Your dad is on his way."

I thought of the night when I heard Danny and his dad fighting. Like thunder on a summer night. Like voices over water.

"Have you caught Wally?" I asked.

"Who's Wally?"

"The dog that was with us."

The cowboy cop looked at the female cop. She shook her head.

"They'll do their best," she said. "Does he have a tag on his collar?"

I nodded.

"Not a license," I said. "Just a tag with his name on it and a phone number."

"Let's make sure we get the dog," the cowboy officer said to the female officer.

She nodded.

"Is that your dog?" he asked.

"Danny's dog."

"You said you weren't his girl, but were you dating Danny?"

"Not really. I grew up next to him."

"But you're all the way up here. Were you heading north?"

"What do you mean? We had to come north to get here from where we live."

"To Canada. Some people go across a border when they get into trouble. Did Danny suggest you go north? Maybe to hide out with him?"

"No, he never said anything like that. Danny's not like that. You're making him out to be too sophisticated or something."

"So you came up to see . . . the statue? Is that what you're telling me?"

"Yes. Today was an in-service at my school. We had a free day, that's all."

"Did Danny act unusual in any way?"

"He seemed a little jumpy, maybe. Not really, though. His phone rang a lot."

"That was us phoning to get in touch with him. We're not trying to be hard on Danny. You know that, right? But something happened in that house and we're trying to sort it out."

"You said they fought."

"That's what it looks like. The house was broken up, mostly the kitchen. We figure the dad might have been drinking. Maybe he was drunker than he knew and Danny got the advantage of him. Pretty ugly scene. If Danny did it, he should have called someone. An ambulance. But it looks like he just left."

"Danny wouldn't do that. He's not like that."

"People do lots of things, Clair. Things you couldn't imagine. I hate to break it to you."

"Danny's not like that."

"Only a few people are really like that, as you say. People get pushed and massaged into things. Everyday people. Did Danny and his dad have a history together? Did Danny talk to you about that? Did they fight a lot, would you say?"

"His dad was violent. That's what people said."

"We've heard some of that. A difficult man, I guess."

"I guess."

He let out a long breath. He seemed satisfied with my answers.

"You hungry at all?" he asked. "Or is your stomach still upset?"

"I'm not hungry."

"Anything else you can tell us about Danny and his dad?"

I shook my head.

"You know it would be wrong to withhold information if you had it. You know that, right?"

I nodded.

"Okay, we're done here for a while."

"Will you check to see if they got Wally? Please? He's not to blame for any of this."

He turned to the female police officer. She nodded.

"I'll check that," she said.

I heard Danny scream a little later. It was a horrible scream. It didn't come from pain or from injury, but from something deep down, something frightened and animal and dark.

"Danny's pretty much coming clean about all this. How are you feeling?" the cowboy cop asked a little later.

"How do you mean he's coming clean? He's confessing?"

"He tried to defend himself from his father. It's pretty much what we thought."

"He admitted that?"

"It was about the dog, partly. His dad wanted the dog out of the house. It was an argument and it escalated."

"Can I see him?"

"No, I'm afraid not."

"For a minute?"

"Not for any time at all, I'm afraid. Danny's in a lot of trouble, Clair. The way you could help is to try to reconstruct the past couple of days."

"There's nothing to reconstruct."

"There's always something to reconstruct," the cowboy-eyed cop said.

He smiled. A real pal.

"Danny needed attention a little lately. That's the only difference."

"How do you mean, needed attention?"

"He was around a lot. He wanted to do things with me."

"Okay. Like this ride up here today?"

I nodded.

"After last night, he probably didn't want to be home much."

I didn't say anything.

"It will be a pretty big story because of the father-son angle. These things usually are."

"He didn't know what to do."

"Did he tell you that?"

"For the last time, I didn't know anything about this. I just know Danny."

I put my hands over my eyes. I suddenly felt exhausted. I could have slept in about one second if I had the chance.

"It happens a lot, you know. Abuse. Then retaliation. You almost can't blame the boy."

"No one deserves to get his head crushed in by a car battery."

"I guess not."

"Is my dad here yet?"

"Soon."

"So, I'm free to go?"

"We want to have a conversation with you and your dad."

"Then?"

"Probably so."

"What's going to happen to Danny?"

"Oh, he'll be transferred downstate. He's just shy of eighteen so he'll be in a young adult population jail. YDSU . . . youth detention."

"Danny won't make it."

"You never know. I'm not saying it will be easy, but sometimes prison pushes someone in a new direction. Sometimes it works."

"Danny's just full of hot air. I mean, he's really not a bad kid."

"A little bit more than hot air, but I get your point."

"Don't you have to prove he did it?"

"He confessed, Clair. He confessed almost at once. He was carrying around a lot of guilt. It was probably a relief to let some of it go."

"This is crazy."

"I'm sure it must feel that way. Is there anything else you can tell us? Good or bad? The best way to help Danny now is to give the full picture. Did you ever see his dad abuse him? Anything like that?"

"No, not specifically. He didn't talk about him, but my dad and Jebby said Elwood was rough."

"Who's Jebby?"

"A guy who grew up in town. He knew Elwood from way back."

"There's a couple of domestic abuse police calls on Elwood. Back in the day. He wasn't a Boy Scout, that's for sure."

I put my head down on the table. I didn't feel like talking anymore. I couldn't think straight anymore.

"Please try to find Wally," I said.

"We're on it."

"And what about his car? Danny's car?"

"We'll tow it out and put it in impound. It's probably already on its way."

The female officer answered a knock at the door. She turned to me.

"Your dad's here," she said.

EIGHTEEN

WE JUST WANTED to go over a few things," the cowboy-eyed cop said to my dad and me.

We no longer sat in the holding room. We sat in someone's office, someone with a big desk and a big window behind it. It was dark now. My dad held my hand. He didn't like cops much, but he also knew not to cross them. He listened.

"Danny's left the building," the cop said. "He's on his way downstate. Concord, I think. Probably Concord."

My dad nodded. He squeezed my hand.

"We believe your daughter, Clair here, we believe she had no previous knowledge of the event in question."

Again my dad nodded. I hated how the cop used such twisted language. I had heard it around me all afternoon. *Previous knowledge. Incarceration. Mitigating circumstances.* They tried to be careful with their language and only made it worse by doing so.

"It's a very sad event. A sad thing to happen in a boy's life. And of course it's a great tragedy for Elwood's extended family."

"Elwood deserved killing if anyone did," my father said, shocking me.

"Now that's an interesting thing to say in this light. In the current situation."

"He beat his wife."

"Still and all. We can't kill people. I think you'd agree with me there, wouldn't you?"

My dad squeezed my hand again. He really didn't like cops. The cop didn't wait for my dad to answer before going on.

"What we wanted to talk about . . . if your daughter remembers anything that might be germane to the case, to Danny's situation, we'd appreciate it if she would get in touch with us. Will you do that?"

"The boy needs care," Dad said. "He's needs some adult help."

"We're agreed on that. He'll get some counseling for sure. I can't go on record here, but I feel sorry for the boy.

I do. I'm sure his rage didn't rise out of nowhere. That will probably be an easy case for the defense to make."

My dad moved his neck around, trying to loosen it.

"It's been a long day," my dad said.

"Okay, you're right. Time to call it a day. I'm sorry to have met you under such difficult circumstances, Clair," the cowboy cop said, rising. "I'll let you get going. It's a long ride home."

I shook hands with the cowboy cop. Dad did too. I asked on the way out if anyone had found Wally and no one met my eyes when they answered no.

In a TV movie, or on a show, I would have bawled my head off as soon as I climbed into our old truck with Dad, but I didn't feel like crying. I felt dead and hard inside. I also felt cold. I asked Dad to turn the heat on high for a while, and he did, even though the night wasn't too bad. We drove awhile without talking. I turned the heat down after we had gone a few miles and Dad cracked his window. It felt like traveling through time. We had the lights from the dashboard, and the lights casting ahead of us, but otherwise the road could have led us anywhere.

"You okay?" Dad asked, and reached over and took my hand.

"Not really okay, Dad."

"You know what I mean. What can I do for you?"

"You think he did it?"

He nodded.

"I'm afraid so," he said. "Just a momentary thing, maybe. He probably argued with his dad and then he saw a way to smash him really hard and he did. I don't know. No one will know. Danny probably doesn't know."

"Was Elwood really brutal with his wife?"

"From all accounts," he said, nodding again. "I guess it was pretty bad. He didn't just have a temper . . . It was more than that. He couldn't stand to be embarrassed or contradicted."

"Things were going pretty well for Danny. I don't know why he put up with it all these years and then snapped one night when things were okay in his life. It doesn't add up."

"Hard to know things like that. You know how when we go hiking or go down a river in the canoe? And how sometimes there are trees dangling over the river?"

"Widow makers. That's what you always called them."

"Yep. One day, in one particular second, those trees give way. Who knows why? I bet if you could figure everything out, every last detail and all the physics of it, then you could see why the tree dropped when it did. But if you can't get the details right, then it just looks like the tree decided to drop for no reason."

"So, we'll never know?"

He wiggled my hand a little.

"Probably not. Not more than we know already."

I shrugged. Wally had been in the kitchen with him. That's what I imagined. That might have been why they fought.

"He was filled with guilt, Clair. I'm sure of that. Don't let people spin it into a big, ghoulish thing. They'll try. He'd just had enough and he broke, that's all. He probably was abused all his life."

"I hate thinking of him in that house alone. With Elwood just doing things over and over to him."

"I know. Me too."

"He used me to be away from it."

"He used you because he liked you and because you were kind. That only credits you, Clair. It's nothing bad or dirty. Nothing you should feel guilty about."

I made him stop near the field where we had lost Wally. I wasn't 100 percent sure it was the same field, because it was dark now and I couldn't see any tire tracks leading out onto the soil. But I stood outside and called awhile, even shook a plastic bag, hoping Wally would think it was food if he was out in the dark, listening. Dad stood next to me and didn't say anything. We drove home mostly in silence after that.

It's obvious, but it's worth saying: A boy can be a dog. Anyone can be a dog. You get what you put into a person, the same way you get what you put into a dog. You fill a dog with hate and that's what you get back. Father Jasper warns about playing tug of war with a dog because, he asks, *What are you teaching it?* You're teaching the dog that you can fight each other, wrestle, and if the dog wins, he thinks he's dominant. Also, on the day when you need a shoe back, and the dog has it, then why shouldn't he think you have to hold a tug of war for it? You taught him it was okay to challenge you.

That was one of the things that happened to Danny, I think. I think his dad played tug of war all his life with his kid, and one day his kid played back.

When we arrived home, we saw yellow police tape strung up at Danny's house. You could tell in a glance that lots of people had been there. The new spring grass in the backyard had been trampled down, and cars had made tire marks up on the lawn where people had parked. The house appeared haunted. It looked dark and worried, almost frowning. That made me wonder, because just that morning I hadn't felt anything about the Stewarts' house one way or the other. It had just been a house, but now that I knew what had gone on inside it, I had a whole different feeling about it. I stood for a while on the back porch watching it. Our house phone rang a lot and there were a ton of messages on my cell, but I left them alone.

My dad came out a little later with two cups of tea. It was a nice night. He handed me one, and he saw I was looking at the Stewarts' house and he asked if I was okay.

"You wonder what goes on in people's houses," I said. "And now I know you can't ever be sure."

"This is just one thing, Clair. Don't generalize it out."

"But it's true, isn't it?"

"That we can't know what goes on in someone else's house? That's true. But we can't know the good things, either. We can't know about the happiness that might be there."

"You don't think he planned it, do you?"

Dad stuck out his lower lip, then shook his head.

"No, I don't think so. They probably got going arguing and then it went to a place it hadn't been before. Maybe it was the first time Danny ever fought back. Maybe knowing you made him realize he deserved not to be hit or assaulted by his father. You and Wally, maybe you made that clear to him."

I felt close to tears again. I thought of Wally wandering the north woods by himself, not knowing what to do or where to go and it tore me up. Then I thought of Danny in a prison somewhere, wearing a jump suit and flip-flops, and it made something burn inside me. I felt like I had something to answer for, that I had set a thing in motion without knowing where it might take us all.

"I saw Mom's statue," I said, throwing it on like you would a piece of brush once you had a fire going well. I didn't care where it landed or how it caught. I felt as though everything needed to come out.

Dad sipped his tea. He sat on the porch railing.

"Okay," he said.

"It's a good statue. It was covered with vines."

"I'm glad you saw it."

"Why didn't you take me to see it?"

He didn't answer right away. When he did, his voice was quiet and thoughtful.

"I don't know exactly," he said. "I could make up a reason now and try to cover for myself, but I don't think either of us is in the mood for that. I guess I told myself it would only stir things up. Besides, they put it up a long time ago. I wasn't even sure it was still there. But that's not really an excuse."

"It is the only statue Mom ever sold."

"I know, Clair."

"That statue is a lot like Mom. Is that why you didn't want to show me?"

"Probably. It's hard to know what your heart wants to tell you sometimes. Your mom used to put her whole self into her projects. It was something I loved about her and admired. I work, but part of me holds back. Your mom wasn't like that. She gave herself completely to the things she did, so seeing that statue would be like seeing her again. Seeing her best part, and maybe I was afraid to do that. I don't know. I haven't sorted it out in my mind completely. I'm sorry now that I didn't take you up there. It was a mistake and I apologize."

"I'm not trying to make you feel bad about it, Dad. I'm trying to understand things. I feel like a lot of things I thought I knew aren't so steady anymore."

"I know. I can see how that would be."

"You think it will be a big story?"

"I think so, Clair. People like reading about this type of thing. It won't go national or anything, but it will be news around here. Probably around the state."

"Am I going to be the girlfriend in the story?"

"I don't think we should talk to anyone in the press, if that's what you mean. Do you? There's no upside to it. It won't help Danny at all. Maybe in the courts we can help him, but in the public eye he's just going to be the crazy kid who tried to kill his father with a car battery."

"I guess you're right. I thought Danny was going to drive right off the end of the world when the police started chasing him. I thought he was going to slam into something like Mom did."

"I'm sorry, Clair."

"He stopped for me. I'm pretty sure of that."

"Deep down, he's a good boy."

"I don't know what he is."

Dad hugged me. He held me in his arms a long time. I knew he was worried about me. He kissed the top of my head.

"You going to be able to sleep?" he asked when he let me go.

"I don't know."

"You just call down the hallway and I'll wake up, okay?"

"Okay."

"Let's get somebody for you to talk to, too. We have insurance for that. Just someone to sort out things. Would you like that?"

"I don't know."

"I'll ask around and get a recommendation. Just to talk with a little. Would that be okay?"

I nodded.

"Come on inside," he said, and I did.

NINETEEN

T HEY FOUND WALLY," my dad told me on the next
Tuesday. "We can take a ride up and get him if you like."

It was early. I was dressed for school.

"What about school?" I asked.

"You can skip it for a day."

"Wally would have to stay with us. I doubt we can put
him over in the Stewarts' yard."

"I know. Why don't we try it and see how it goes?"

I knew it was something Dad proposed to make me
feel better. He was worried about me, and I understood
that.

"Don't you have to work today?" I asked Dad as we walked out to the truck.

"I'm taking a sick day."

"Wow."

"Let's just see how it goes. You said Wally was doing better."

"Much better."

"So, who knows?"

We followed the same route that Danny and I had taken. We found Wally at the SPCA in Bolston. It wasn't more than a glorified trailer, but it had runs in back and even a corral where a horse came over to watch us. A little old lady with a volunteer tag on her smock made us fill out some paperwork and pay thirty dollars for boarding the dog. She said the police had dropped him off. Two hikers had found Wally out on a hiking trail running loose, so they tied a bungee cord to him and brought him down to town. They turned him over to the police, and that's how Wally arrived at the SPCA. The police had known whom to call.

"He was some hungry, too," the woman said, leading us into the back. "Almost ate us out of house and home. But he's in good shape. None the worse for wear."

I started to cry when I saw Wally.

He reared up on the cage door, crazy to see us, and

he stood nearly as tall as my dad. I told him off, but he didn't listen, and I had to squeeze through the door by pushing his weight away. When I finally got inside with him, he started to whine. It was the old whining, the sound I used to hear late at night in the winter, and I put my arms around his neck and tucked my face into his fur.

"I'm sorry," I said to him.

The old lady and my dad didn't do anything or say anything. I held on to Wally and felt my heart turning and ripping, and Danny was mixed up in it, and sorrow for things I couldn't name.

We stopped at the fly-fisherman statue on the way home. It looked better now that the vines had finally fallen away from gravity and the wind blowing. The wind turned the statue and sometimes the lower gears moved. It was clever the way my mom had constructed it. The statue contained motion but was still a statue, and that required a good eye and a steady hand to bring off.

"It's bigger than I remembered it," my dad said, circling it slowly. "More dramatic, too."

"It's a pretty cool statue."

"Your mother had talent. She didn't have all the follow-through in the world, but she had talent."

"Who bought this?"

"I'm trying to remember. It was a commission or a contest, I'm not sure which. She was very excited and she stayed up here for a week installing it. They did a little ceremony when they unveiled it. They called it an unveiling, but it wasn't like it was covered or anything. Your mom was happy."

"Was I here?"

"Of course," he said, appearing surprised that I'd ask. "Where else would you have been?"

"I don't know."

"You were just a toddler. Maybe a little older than that. We have pictures of the day somewhere. Probably up in that plastic crate thingy in the sewing room."

"I'd like to see them."

Dad nodded, but his eyes stayed on the statue. He made a full circle.

"We could clean it up for her," he said. "Oil it and polish it a little. You want to do that?"

"When?"

"Right now. We have the day off. We can get the stuff at a hardware store. There must be one around here somewhere."

"You'll need a ladder."

"Maybe. But if we park right next to it, we can probably climb up high enough to do it some good."

My head felt light and dizzy. I didn't want him to do it to satisfy me, to inoculate me against feelings I might have regarding Danny. My brain couldn't follow a straight line about it.

"I'd like to see Danny," I said.

He looked at me. He nodded.

"Of course."

"He's alone."

"I think you should see him when you're ready."

"Soon."

"I'll look into it," Dad said. "What it takes and so on."

"And I want to train Wally so that he's a great dog."

"Okay. How about the statue? You want to clean it?"

I nodded. Dad looked at me seriously for a while, then finally crossed his eyes at me and made a face. I didn't laugh or acknowledge the face at first, but he kept doing it until I made a face back. We both laughed, and it had been a while since that happened.

A disciplined dog is a free dog, Father Jasper says. That's why Danny wasn't free. No one had taught him to be disciplined, and now they had caught him and locked him up. He wasn't much different from a dog.

We did a good job, a thorough job, of cleaning the statue. We pulled the pickup next to it, and I climbed on the roof to get at the highest parts. We polished everything and greased the gears. Dad said he could remember Mom working on the statue, how she had suddenly seen its shape emerge from the pile of bike parts, and how excited she had been when the unveiling had taken place. A town band played at the event, and the head of the select board had read a short speech about the value of art in a community. Mom had been excited and happy. It was one of the good days, Dad said. One of the best.

When we finished, we stepped back and judged our work. The statue gleamed and the slightest breeze made the parts move. It was only when we got ready to leave that I saw Mom's signature on the I-beam. It would have been impossible to sign the statue itself, given the thinness of most of the parts, but Mom had signed near the foot of the angler. I showed Dad. He put his fingers on it and smiled a sad smile.

"I didn't know she had done that," he said. "Funny I missed that all these years."

"She must have been proud of it."

"She was. She loved this statue. I'm glad you came to see it."

"Do I look like Mom? Mrs. Cummings says I do."

He put his arm around me.

"Sure you do."

"She was prettier than I am."

"No, that's not true. You're very pretty, Clair. Your mom thought you were the most beautiful baby she had ever known. She said you were going to be a heartbreaker."

"Mom was very pretty."

"She was."

"I'm glad we cleaned the statue."

"So am I. I feel bad we ignored it all these years. I ignored it, I should say."

"It gleams. And when the wind turns it, it's really something."

"That's your mom standing there. I mean, not really. I guess it's a male fisherman, but your mom is in the parts. I don't know if she meant to do it, but she left her stamp there. Do you see it too?"

I nodded. We watched it awhile longer, then we drove home.

TWENTY

ON THE BUS a few days later, Cow Bell said he saw Danny on the news.

"Bonked his dad with a car battery! That's some kind of strange. My mom said they had a picture of you on the news too, but only for a second. I guess they did an arraignment, right? I think that's what she saw."

Cow Bell hung over the back of the seat in front of me. His breath smelled like pretzels and milk. He wore a camo cap pulled down close to his ears.

"Leave me alone, Cow Bell," I said. "I don't feel like talking."

"He left him on the ground to die, that's what I heard. Right on the kitchen floor."

"Shut up, Cow Bell."

The bus stopped. More kids climbed on. Cow Bell seemed to think about the next way to approach the subject while the other kids found their seats.

"You think he'll go to prison?" he asked when the bus started moving again.

"He's in prison now, Cow Bell. If you hit someone in the head, you go to prison. That's just the way it is. It's not like in the movies when people get away with stuff."

"Dag, that's crazy. He'll come back all tatted up and you'll be some prison wife kind of thing living in a trailer somewhere. It's wild."

Cow Bell slid down into his seat. I tried to read my French textbook, but I couldn't concentrate. Cow Bell pulled out his cell phone and played a game. His archenemy, Larry Grieg, wasn't on the bus for some reason.

Holly met me at the bus stop. She didn't often do that, but today was a big day.

"You were on the news last night! Did you see it? I tried to call about a million times, but you didn't answer!"

She carried her books against her chest. I knew she was dying for information, for any gossip I could give her, but I didn't want to do that to Danny. I felt protective of him, and I told her I didn't want to talk about it.

"Things have been crazy. We went back up to bring Wally home. They found him on a hiking trail."

"Well, that's good at least. Right? That's something. Are you going to keep him?"

"I think so. I hope so."

Then she had to get to the topic du jour.

"Seriously?" she said as if she were merely answering a question someone else asked. "I can't believe Danny could do something like that. I mean, can you? Can you believe a guy you dated is now in prison?"

"I didn't date him, Holly. Don't even say that to people."

"Well, whatever it was. He's now in prison. Danny Stewart. It's wild."

I stopped and looked at her.

"I need you to help me," I said. "I need you to help me protect Danny. I don't want everyone talking about him and making fun of him. He doesn't deserve that. Promise me you won't let it be this lurid thing that happened to someone we know. He's real, Holly. He's in real pain, I bet. We both know Danny wouldn't do something like that if he didn't have to."

Holly nodded. She looked me dead in the eyes and then she nodded hard as if she finally understood. She put her arm through my arm and walked me to the school entrance.

* * *

I got away to see Mrs. Cummings between third and fourth periods. She was down in her office shelling peas. She looked nice; she seemed brushed up and carefully dressed for a change. As soon as I walked in, she hugged me. I nearly broke down being in her arms. After a little she made me sit and gave me some broccoli tops she had cut up for the raw bar.

"You okay?" she asked.

I shrugged.

"I can't imagine you are. You can't blame the kid, honey. He just fought back is all. You can't blame him for fighting back finally."

"He almost killed him."

"He hit him, that's all. Isn't that right? That's what was reported. I know how people will go on, but that's all that happened. A person can't take and take and take forever. No one can. If he had been a little older, maybe he could have moved out. He probably didn't know his options and he had no one to help him at anything except you."

"I didn't help him. I may have made the situation worse."

She grabbed my hand.

"No, no, no. Don't blame yourself that way. That doesn't get you anywhere you want to go."

I realized she wasn't wearing her gray cardigan. That was what had changed.

"What are you dressed up for?" I asked. I ate two broccoli tops, but they tasted too green for the mood I was in.

"My hubby is taking me for a ride on the *Mount Washington*."

"The boat?"

"On Lake Winnipesaukee. It's a company thing for him and I wanted to look nice."

"You do look nice. Really nice."

"Well, I do what I can. So anyway, sweetie, don't turn your fellow into some sort of gangster. He was just fighting to survive."

"I know."

"My husband knew Elwood Stewart from back in the day. He talked about him when we saw it on the news last night. He said Elwood was a devil, a real devil. Of course that's not an excuse to cause him physical harm, but it provides context, now, doesn't it?"

"Danny's not a mean kid."

She nodded. Then to change the subject I told her about going up and seeing the statue. She listened. She smiled when I related how my father had helped too, and the statue looked almost new.

"Well, isn't that something? Good for you. Your mom

would be proud. Something nice can come out of even the worst situation, see? I may get my grumpy old husband to drive me up there someday to look at it. I'd like to see it. I'd like to have a picnic right beside it."

"It looks good now. It turns in the wind."

The bell for fourth period rang.

"I've got to go," I said.

She hugged me once more.

"Stay brave," she said. "Remember, you know in your heart what's what, and don't let people try to talk that away."

She took a mint and tossed it in her mouth. Then she washed her hands with sanitizer. She put the peas on a tray next to the broccoli tops and carried them toward the cafeteria.

Holly rode the bus home with me after school. Technically she wasn't supposed to do that unless we had a permission slip, but the driver, Lenny, never checked, and to him Holly was simply one more brat to drop off. She sat next to me, and Cow Bell left us alone.

We didn't talk about Danny. Not then. She told me about a boy she had met from the next town over, John something-or-other, who worked at the rock-climbing barn in Plymouth and was really cute, climber cute, with wiry legs and arms and hair down to his shoulders. Then she told me about a skirt her mother had found for her at the Gap, and it made her look short, everything made her look short, but it worked pretty well. Blue with polka dots, but not old-lady polka dots, she said, young polka dots.

It was nice listening to her. I liked not having to talk. It was like hearing rain.

Cow Bell got off ahead of us at Riley's convenience store. I realized, for him, it was a pretty good day. He rode back and forth to school without being terrorized by Larry Grieg.

"See you, Cow Bell," I said, because he was Cow Bell and no one else was going to say goodbye to him.

"See ya," he said.

He walked off. I watched him pick up an intact set of soda can plastic rings, loop it together so it was one ring, and try to break it behind his back. He tried until he was out of sight, but I didn't see the rings snap.

We bought a large bag of plain M&M's and ate them as we walked toward my house. I gave Holly credit: She stayed off the Danny topic unless I brought it up. She told me an involved story about a girl we knew named Tabitha whose boyfriend broke up by sending her a picture of himself in bed with another girl. I didn't pay close attention.

"I keep thinking about that day at the Peppermint Bridge," I said eventually, when her story about Tabitha wound down. "How nice Danny was that day and how happy he seemed. He must have been torn up inside more than we knew."

"Poor kid."

"I'm supposed to be able to go down and see him sometime soon."

"In prison?"

I nodded.

"Wow," she said. "That's going to be strange."

"It's just Danny."

"Do you think you're in love with him?"

Holly looked at me. She held out the open mouth of the bag toward me.

"I don't know. I don't even think I know what that means. We talk about who loves who, but I don't know what people mean by it. Not really."

"You said, though, that you had a great day with him before he got arrested."

"I did. It was a nice day."

"It's all so bizarre."

"Mrs. Cummings said people can't just take and take and take forever. They have to fight back."

"She's right," Holly said, putting M&M's into her mouth. "No one can."

When we reached the Stewarts' house, I saw someone had put an old car battery on top of the mailbox. It took a second to make sense of it. What was a car battery doing on the mailbox? I wondered for an instant before it clicked. I handed Holly my backpack.

"Hold this, will you?" I asked.

She did. I lifted the car battery off the mailbox. It was heavy. I had to put it on the ground and readjust my hands before I could lift it again. I carried it to our backyard. I had to hold it against my chest and stomach and it rubbed dirt all over me. I put it with some junk parts my dad had for the truck.

"People are jerks," Holly said as she handed me back my backpack. "Seriously."

"Danny's an easy target."

"Still."

"People like to pick on someone. It makes them feel bigger or more important. I've seen it a lot lately. Danny's situation made me see it."

Holly held out the M&M's bag to me again.

"I'm turning into a cow, swear to God," she said. "Keep these away from me."

"Even if you beg?"

"Especially if I beg. I'm going to grow out of everything I own."

We climbed the porch to the back door. Wally squirmed and yipped a little from his crate in the kitchen. I opened the door and told him I was home.

* * *

I cleaned off our back porch after Holly's brother picked her up around five. It wasn't a conscious thing, but maybe it had to do with seeing the battery over at Danny's house. I had gone out on the porch to say goodbye, and the weather was soft and warm and the sun seemed reluctant to set. So walking Wally out to his bathroom place, I lifted an old end table off the porch, and that seemed to set something free inside of me. I carried it down and put it in the driveway, out of the way, but where we could load it into a Dumpster or into the truck to take to the transfer station. Then I went back and carried down more junk. I tied Wally to the porch post so he could hang out with me.

It *was* junk. I couldn't blame it all on my mom. Some of it was car or motorcycle parts my dad had jammed there, and some of it belonged to me. I had three Hula-Hoops —all broken in some way—that I had been too lazy to discard. I had a cruddy bike that needed more repair than it was ever going to see in this world, and a swing set, half dismantled, that my father had wedged there to keep it out of the weather before he could erect it for me. That had been years before.

The work made me warm, even though the temperature was in the fifties. I got into it and before long I had made a serious dent in the collected trash. When I walked down to the growing pile near the driveway, I observed that the house wasn't too bad if you gave it a proper cleaning. The porch almost looked gracious—if you looked at it in a certain way—and I wondered how we had let it get so bad, how we had walked past it day in and day out without ever stopping to consider what we were doing. It made me uneasy to think that we had been so lazy or so blind about what we had done.

I was sweeping the cleaned-off porch with the big push broom by the time my dad got home. He climbed out of his truck and looked around at the assembled junk, then up to the porch, then back to the junk.

"You've been busy," he said. "What got into you?"

He bent down and petted Wally when he came up the steps. Wally stayed quiet and let him.

"I got tired of looking at it, I guess."

"Well, it looks a heck of a lot better, doesn't it?"

"I'd say so."

"Funny how things gang up in a spot."

"I didn't fix anything for dinner. I got involved in this."

"That's okay. We should have done this a long time ago, I suppose."

He put his things in the house and I heard him run water. I heard him crack a beer. He came out a few minutes later and took the broom from my hand. He put the beer on the railing and looked at me.

"You okay?" he asked.

I nodded.

"School okay?"

"It was okay."

"I worried about you today. But it went okay?"

I nodded again.

He put his arms around me and hugged me hard for a moment.

"This is all going to be okay, you know," he said. "All in the fullness of time. Time works, believe me."

"Yep."

"Just go slow."

"I will."

He let me go and then took a look at the porch.

"We could paint this, you know. It would look a thousand times better with a coat of paint."

"Okay."

"Maybe this is our summer to clean up around here."

"Maybe so."

Then he swept, working the broom hard, while I used the big dustpan and scooped up the debris. We worked until we could hardly see anymore. A couple of fireflies came out and flashed, their signals burning like a hand holding a cigarette and waving goodbye.

It might have been one night; it might have been a thousand nights.

In my bedroom, I waved my hand across my waist. Wally sat.

I made a down motion and he went on his belly, his eyes watching me. He had a new collar made from a colorful weave of black and red and a little purple. It looked great on him. I had shampooed him after his adventure on his own and his fur still glistened. He looked healthy and handsome. He was an impressive dog now that he was cleaned up. His rabies tag hung in the middle of his chest, a spot of silver on his black body. Dad had paid to make sure his shots were up to date.

I pushed my hand at his eyes. "Stay," I said.

Then I walked away and he stayed where I left him. I watched him for a little while. He watched me.

Eventually I squatted down, slapped my leg, and said, "Come."

He lumbered over into my arms, nearly knocking me down. Then I got him to sit next to me and I held him for a long time, my forehead against his chest, my arm over his back.

I whispered to him that I loved him. I whispered that he was the best dog in the world. I called him a secret name, Gold Moon, because one night when I woke up feeling frightened, I saw the moon streaming in through my window and it reflected off Wally's coat. For a second he didn't seem like a dog. Or rather, he seemed better than a dog, seemed like the greatest dog that ever lived, and I whispered "Gold Moon" to him. It sounded corny and stupid, but the moon continued to move and light ran slowly down his body. It felt like all the planets and every single thing swirling in space had conspired to send that single ray of light through my window to find him. Like the universe's flashlight. He stayed still, his head up, and looked at me, and I thought of him out on that pole, his body chilled with ice and vapor, and I imagined the light as his reward, as some sort of cosmic payment for his suffering. It had given him nobility, all that suffering, and I cried quietly watching him.

But now in my room, I stayed next to Wally, and we didn't do anything special. He was my dog.

TWENTY-ONE

A DOG IS PART of heaven, Father Jasper says. A dog will lead you to heaven if you let him.

Three weeks later we drove down to Concord on my dad's motorcycle, because it was warm and sunny out and my dad couldn't resist. I didn't mind using the motorcycle, because I didn't want to have to talk on the way down. My dad wasn't certain it was a good idea that I see Danny, but I argued that I had to see him at some point, so why not now? If we had taken the truck, I knew, he would have felt the need to lecture me and tell me how to handle things, how to approach Danny, and I was grateful we could skip that.

It was nice riding, anyway. I clung to my dad's back and we drove at the speed limit and the Harley ran smooth and powerful beneath us. Spring was a thin line of warm days and I saw everything green and perfect on either side of I-93. We passed the Pemigewasset and the Merrimack, both of the rivers like flashes of bright rope, and for a while, over my dad's shoulder, I watched a pair of red-tailed hawks circling. Being on the bike blocked everything. It was all sensation, all speed and impressions, and so when we finally turned into the parking lot of the Concord Correctional Facility, I felt like I was waking from a dream.

"Pretty riding day," Dad said, swinging off after me.

I pulled off my helmet. I bent to check my hair. It stuck up like a broom.

"How did the bike sound?" I asked, because he liked talking about the bike.

"Sounded good. Better than it did last season."

"I won't be long."

"I'm coming in with you, Clair."

"I need to do this on my own."

"It's a prison. Lots of dirtbags in here."

"I know. I can handle it. I've handled Jebby all my life."

I meant it as a joke. I handed him my helmet. He shook his head.

"I'll let you talk to Danny on your own, but I'm coming in to make sure things go okay. I'm not debating that, Clair."

I shrugged.

We headed toward the building. All cinder block. All razor wire.

We had to wait for lunch to finish. We sat in an ugly lobby on uncomfortable chairs and leafed through yellowed magazines. People came and went. Cops came and went. I heard a lot of keys, a lot of buzzing, a lot of loud talking. Someone had a television on in another part of the waiting room and we heard daytime talk shows and commercials. The commercials were always louder than the regular programming. The building bounced sound everywhere. It was like being inside a can.

Sitting in the lobby, waiting and reading, I thought of Wally. I thought of how Wally had been on his chain, outside, alone. Prisons are posts in the ground where we tie up troublesome dogs. That's what it felt like to me. It was pretty obvious, but that didn't mean it wasn't true.

* * *

"Clair?" a woman asked.

She wore squeaky shoes and a lanyard around her neck. She carried a clipboard.

"Hi," I said, standing.

My dad stood too.

"Here to see Danny Stewart, aren't you?"

"Yes."

"Good. He's been looking forward to it. I'm his case-worker. My name is Paula."

She shook hands with us both. She smiled. She must just have had her lunch, because her lipstick looked fresh and shiny, as if she had reapplied it recently. She had gray hair cut short and she wore sneakers. She looked like a gym teacher.

Dad hugged me. Then I followed Paula past the check-in desk and into the cinder blocks.

I didn't know what to expect. Anything I knew about prison visits came from television. I thought I'd have to sit on one side of a Plexiglas window, Danny on the other, and we would speak through a phone, or a hole in the glass, and a bunch of other visitors would be doing the same thing on either side of us. But it wasn't like that. It wasn't nearly as dramatic as all that.

Paula led me into a small conference room, and she nodded at a guard on the other side of the room. That guard, a large man who had an enormous potbelly hanging over his belt, opened the door and held it back. A second later Danny stepped inside.

"Hi, Clair," he said.

"Hi, Danny."

He wore an orange jump suit. His sideburns were gone.

"Henry here is going to stay in the room while you two talk. No touching, thanks. No physical contact. If the conversation turns inappropriate, Henry will step in and end the visit. Is that clear? Danny, we talked about the ground rules. Keep them in mind. I'll give you about a half-hour. If you don't want to use the full half-hour, just tell Henry and he'll call me. Does that make sense to everyone? We all on the same page? Is that clear?"

I nodded. Danny nodded too.

Paula left. Henry slumped against the door and crossed his arms. It felt weird to have to talk in front of him, but he didn't seem to care about anything in the world.

I pulled out a chair and sat. Danny sat. I felt lightheaded and slightly detached from my body. I felt like I was going to be sick. But then I took some deep breaths. I tried to focus on Danny.

"How's Wally doing?" Danny asked.

"He's great. He knows down-stay, stay, come, and sit, and, well, you know."

"Cool. I'm glad to hear that."

"I'm trying to get him to catch a Frisbee. It's not easy. I've been working with him a lot, though."

"You can have my car," he said in a non sequitur.

It was Danny being nervous. I ignored it.

"You okay?" I asked. "In here, I mean?"

"Yep. It's okay here. Not that bad."

"Will they keep you here, or transfer you someplace else?"

"Not sure yet. My lawyer is working all that out."

"So you have a lawyer?"

"State appointed."

"Good."

"Seriously, Clair, you can have my car. I'm not going to be using it for a long time."

"I don't want your car, Danny."

"It's going to sit and not be used. I'll sell it to you for a dollar. If it's still running when I get out, you can sell it back to me for a dollar."

"Doesn't somebody in your family want it?"

He looked down at the table. He appeared much younger without the sideburns. He had lost weight, too, and the jump suit swam all over him.

"Sorry," I said.

"My family isn't all that interested in me at the moment. I don't get a lot of visitors."

"Sorry."

"Will you think about it anyway?"

I nodded. It was easier to go along with it than argue it out.

"Okay, Danny."

Then we didn't say anything. Henry, the guard, rubbed his back against the wall. It made a grating sound.

"I don't know why," Danny said eventually. "I don't know why I did it."

"You don't have to explain anything."

"I kind of want to. But I don't have an answer, Clair. It felt like I had a robot inside me and the robot was going to do whatever it wanted and I tried to shut it down, but it kept moving even when I told it to stop. I've got a counselor and that's working okay. I'm talking it out with him. Some guys in the block, they say the devil gets inside people and makes them do bad things, but I don't believe them."

"What's going to happen to you? Do you know what your sentence might be?"

"Not really. I've heard a whole range of things. It's probably going to be attempted murder. I'm not counting on anything."

"I'm sorry about it all, Danny."

"No reason for you to be sorry, Clair. You were nice to me. You were nicer to me than any other person in my life. That's the truth."

"It didn't seem to help you much."

He shrugged. His hands jittered a little on his lap.

"He threw some hot water at Wally. Hot water that he was boiling for his instant coffee," he said. "I told him to stop it. He did it again just to be a jerk."

"And that started it?"

"That was the first round. A little later he came up to my room and he grabbed me by the ear. I was in bed and half asleep and he kind of lifted me out of bed by the ear. He said to put the dog out. I had Wally fixed up in the kitchen on a blanket, but Dad got it into his head that the dog should be out. Then he let me go. So I went down and I put Wally out, and when I came back, Dad flicked hot water at me. He'd been drinking. He said I was just a dog too, and he had half a mind to tie me out with Wally. Something drunk and stupid like that. He kept flicking spoonfuls of hot water at me, so I tried to go past, to go to bed, and he grabbed me by the ear again and I swung at him."

"Sorry, Danny."

Danny looked at Henry. Then he looked back at me.

"I guess I surprised him, because he lurched over to one side and slipped on the water. He knocked over a bunch of things and turned the kitchen table over. He went down hard, drunken hard, and then I lifted the car battery and dropped it on him. They're trying to say I slammed it down on him, but I don't think I did, Clair. I think I just dropped it on him."

"It doesn't matter, Danny. It wasn't your fault."

"He didn't even have his hands up to protect himself. He was stunned, I suppose, to find himself on the floor. I dropped it on him and the corner of the battery hit him right above the brow and there was a ton of blood. So much blood."

I wanted to hold his hand, to do something to give him comfort, but that was against the rules.

"I took off then. I went up to the P&H Truck Stop over in Vermont and I just drank coffee. Then I texted you about going somewhere and that was that. I tried to ignore it. I hoped it would go away."

"Who found your father?"

"He dialed nine-one-one himself. I don't know how he did it, but he did. He woke up about midmorning and he said his son had tried to kill him. That's why they came after us so hard."

"It freaked me out, I have to say. The cops, I mean."

"I know. I'm sorry about that. I just couldn't talk about it. I couldn't do anything. I had such a good day with you and Wally that I pretended nothing had happened back home. Sorry, Clair. I know that wasn't fair."

"It's okay, Danny."

"Dad hasn't been in touch. I don't think he will get in touch."

I nodded.

That was it. Paula came back a few minutes later. It didn't feel as though a half-hour had passed. She still had her clipboard.

"Sorry, guys," she said. "Time's up."

Danny stood. I stood too.

"I'm learning to play the guitar," he said on his way out. "The blues."

"Of course."

"Think about the car."

Then Henry closed the door and I followed Paula back to my father.

"Okay?" Dad asked when I came back to the waiting room.

I shrugged. Then I folded into him and couldn't stop crying for a long time.

About three weeks later a bill of sale came from the Concord prison conveying the car to me for the price of one dollar. Danny attached a note saying he would accept the dollar on credit. He provided the VIN. I realized, reading it, that he must have had the number memorized.

* * *

When I showed the note from Danny to my dad, he shook his head. We had just finished dinner. He read it with his pair of glasses down on his nose. The reflection of the paper made his eyes look as though they were covered with Post-it notes.

"We don't want to get involved in all that," he said, placing the note on the table. "Not until the dust settles and maybe not even then. I'm hearing that Elwood will be coming home pretty soon. We ought to let things go back to normal. As normal as they can be."

"His dad isn't going to be on his side."

"You don't know that, Clair. Look, it's not good any way you slice it. It's nice of Danny to think of you and to want to give you his car, but Danny's not in a position to give things away."

"It's his car."

"Maybe. Maybe it's registered under his dad's name. I don't want to get involved and you shouldn't either. I know it's hard, but put your attention somewhere else. Danny is going to have to make do on his own now."

"We could keep his car for him. Just put a tarp over it. Not drive it or anything."

Dad took off his glasses and put them on top of the note on the table.

"You've got a good heart, Clair. I know that. But this isn't our mess to clean up. It isn't, sweetheart. Elwood might show up and say, *Hey, where's the car?* That's prob-ably likely. Then we're right in the middle of things. *You're* right in the middle of things. It might appear to his dad that you're trying to get something out of this. I know it's hard, but try not to invest too much in Danny. I don't mean to be cruel. You shouldn't be cruel, but you have to understand he's drowning and he's going to reach out and grab at anything to keep afloat."

"So we let him drown?" I asked, and felt hot tears come into my eyes.

"No, but we make sure we don't jump into the pool beside him. That's the first rule of water safety. You don't make a bad situation worse by risking your own life. You know what I'm saying, Clair. I know you do."

We didn't talk for a second. Then I asked if I should write Danny back.

"You can if you want, Clair. I'm sure he'd like hearing from you. Just keep things on the level. Take things easy right now, if you see what I mean. You don't want to fall into his drama."

Talking to my dad usually made me feel good, but I went upstairs feeling squirmy in my stomach. I brought Wally with me and we practiced sitting and paw and down for a while in my room. I gave him biscuits when he per-formed properly. He was getting good. Sometimes he started the behavior before I even made the hand motion to initiate it. I knew working with him was tied up with Danny, but I still couldn't even say what I thought about Danny. Now and then I thought about kissing him, and the bowling and dancing. I tried not to do that.

Holly called later and I talked to her for a while. She liked discussing the whole Danny situation, but someone — probably her parents, but maybe a counselor — somewhere probably told her to lay off it unless I brought it up, because she talked like a dragon sitting on a treasure trove. She talked about everything but Danny, except you knew the pile of Danny bones under her belly amounted to her real treasure. She needed to bring me closer, to get me talking, and I hated that she pulled me in, but I also wanted to talk about him. So I talked, and I hated myself as I talked, but I talked anyway.

"I still can't believe you dated a guy in prison," she said when I told her about the car offer.

"He wasn't in prison," I said, though I knew she would tell it that way around school. "He's in prison now."

"But you were, like, with a felon. That's just crazy. We both hung around with him."

"I know."

"I shouldn't call him a felon. That sounds horrible."

I looked at myself in the mirror over my dresser. Wally watched me from my bed. He had his mouth open, panting, and occasionally he tried to smell something on the evening air leaking into my bedroom from the window. I stared at my mouth whenever it moved. I thought it moved too much, like it had to give each word an extra pat as it left my tongue.

"It's attempted patricide," I said, stealing the word from an account in the newspaper. "Officially, I guess. It's kind of a ridiculous word, but it's accurate."

"People are fascinated with Danny. Everyone pretends he was some big friend of theirs now, but when he was around no one cared."

"Well, he wasn't around that much."

"Still. He's like a celeb for trying to kill his dad. I really think people admire him in a weird way."

"I wonder how Danny goes on from here."

"Do you think he'll be in prison a long time?"

"Not that long. I don't know. He tried to kill his father but the whole situation was bad. The lawyers will try to explain what went on in that house."

"Did you ever see his dad be brutal?"

I shook my head. Then I realized Holly couldn't hear that.

"No," I said.

"Will you be a witness?"

"I guess so."

"God, that is sooooo weird."

I was still talking to Holly when I saw Elwood's pickup

pull into the Stewarts' yard. It was dark so I couldn't see much, but I stood back from the window and lowered my shades.

Wally heard the pickup door shut and he turned his head to listen. He still panted, a tiny string of drool dripping from his flews. I wiped it away with a tissue, and after I threw the tissue away, I watched Elwood walk up toward his front door. His image was indistinct in that light, but I knew his size and shape. He wore black, or navy, and he looked bent over somehow, as if he couldn't straighten his back after a long drive. He had no light to work with, so he fumbled for a while trying the lock, I guessed. Finally he walked out to the front yard and went to stand under the streetlight, his head down, his hand sorting keys. He looked like a shadow—like a shadow that had come to life and walked around but had nothing inside him. Eventually he must have found the key he needed, because he walked back toward the front door more quickly now, his dark clothes gobbled up by the increasing night. Then little by little the lights came on in the Stewart house, and I saw him passing by windows, slowly, finding his way. The light switched on in the kitchen, the place where Elwood had finally met his match. I didn't wait for the other lights to come on. I shut my shades and went over to Wally and pulled him almost on top of me, letting his weight keep me from floating up in the air.

TWENTY-TWO

NOTHING HAPPENED for a while. School drifted away and I was glad to be done with it, although I missed seeing Mrs. Cummings. Then one Saturday Holly's brother, Jack, took us to the Battengate Mall. He complained the whole way, saying it was bogus that he had to give us rides places just because he was older and wanted to use the car. He was a tall, thin kid who had lousy skin and lousy posture. He was a geek in a lot of ways, and he participated in robot gladiator contests with about six kids from the high school. His eyes kept meeting my eyes in the rearview mirror, and he always cleared his throat after they did.

He dropped us at Old Navy and told us to meet him

in two hours at the same spot. Then he drove off to go to a nearby electronics hobby store. Holly rolled her eyes when he drove away.

"I swear wolves brought him to live with us," she said, leading me inside. "He's such an idiot."

"At least he gave us a ride."

"It was either give us a ride or he couldn't use the Jeep. Don't give him more credit than he deserves. He's such a nerd."

It felt good to be in the mall. It felt normal and I didn't even mind Holly's incessant chatter. She wanted to buy shorts, something good for the summer, but she complained that her legs were too fat and shorts never looked good on a short person. We shopped Old Navy hard. She found a pair that looked okay, but the price was higher than she liked, and she hemmed and hawed for a while before finally handing them to the checkout girl. She really wanted two tops she found on the discount rack, but she said her mother would kill her if she came back with tops instead of shorts.

"I love little plastic bags from the mall," she said when we left. "I just do."

We shopped a drugstore and Victoria's Secret, and then wandered around in the center court, looking at food options, before settling on pizza slices and Diet Cokes. We sat next to a new car that was set up on blocks and slowly turned on a pedestal. The side mirror flashed every time light hit it in a certain way, and I couldn't tell if it was intended or not. It was a Ford of some sort and it reminded me of the car in the bowling alley on my day with Danny. Meanwhile, Holly talked nonstop, her mouth gobbling down the pizza without interrupting her speech. She had to start work as a nanny soon, thus the shorts, and she already hated the two girls who would be left in her charge.

"I mean, they are soooooo spoiled," she said, her lips blowing on the pizza to cool it, "that they don't even pick up their toys. They have a room that's called Toy Land, I swear, and they're allowed to leave anything out that they want to play with. Their mom, Nancy, thinks it spurs creativity, but I think it's just nasty and lazy."

"At least she doesn't make you clean it up."

"Not yet, but that's coming. I'm her little slave for the summer. She gets me to do everything while she's off playing tennis in her tiny white skirts. She goes out the door and the kids' heads start revolving around on their shoulders. Demon children. My mom calls their mom Fancy Nancy. She knows her from a couple of clubs or something."

"It's a job, at least."

"It's slavery. I'm a kid and I need work, so they rip me off. Everyone does that. And I'm responsible for the two little brats. Plus, my whole world is just girls. The mom, my mom, two girls, you. I need a man!"

It made me laugh to hear her say it. She cocked her head and laughed too, her little coyote laugh that always made me laugh harder. It was a wheezy laugh, kind of insucking breath, and she saved it for moments when she liked to make me crack up.

Then a weird thing happened. I saw Danny. It took me a couple heartbeats to realize it wasn't Danny, but for that brief interval between seeing and knowing, I thought it was. It turned out to be another boy about his age and size, but I had a full moment when I thought, *There he is.* It was a kid coming out of Bed Bath & Beyond, and his head was turned away from me, but something about his body, his posture, reminded me of Danny. I opened my mouth to say something, but then the kid turned and I saw I was mistaken. Holly saw my expression and she turned to follow my sight line, and when she turned back she said, "What? You look like you saw a ghost."

"Nothing. I thought I knew that kid."

"Weird."

"You aren't kidding," I said.

She took a bite of pizza and sloshed down a squirt of Diet Coke from her straw.

"Did you guys ever mess around? You and Danny? I never really got to the bottom of that."

"What do you mean?"

"You know what I mean, Clair Taylor. You know."

I thought of kissing Danny that day by the bowling alley. I thought of that a lot.

"I wouldn't call it messing around. We kissed. I told you all that."

"I thought you might be holding out on me."

"I didn't even think that way about him. He was more like a friend, but then sometimes he almost seemed like a boyfriend. I don't know."

"I can see what you mean," she said, dabbing at her mouth with a napkin. "He was a boy, but he was also Danny. I get it. Thing is, you have a little bit of a reputation because you were dating this guy who tried to off his dad."

"A bad reputation?" I asked, my stomach folding in half.

"No, no, I just meant people look at you a little differently. They say, wow, I didn't know Clair was this wild woman. You know what I'm saying."

I didn't know what she meant. I had no idea.

I said, "Nothing is as dramatic as you think it's going to be. Life isn't like that."

"I know. I hear you on that."

She burped. It was a loud burp. Then she looked around and did her coyote laugh.

"Clair, that's gross!" she said, blaming it on me. "I wish you'd stop doing things like that!"

I blushed but Holly was pretty funny.

We walked down to the pet store at the end of the mall. We always went there. It was closed, though. Someone had put up a sign that said OUT OF BUSINESS. The lights in the pens—where they used to keep puppies—still shone brightly in the window. It looked strange, wood chips scattered around, the lights on, but no animals.

"How do you close down a pet store?" I asked, feeling anxious at the thought of it. "I mean, it's not like a furniture store or something. You can't just junk all the stock."

"Oh, I'm sure they found places to put them."

"But where?"

"Someplace, Clair. Don't worry about it."

But I did worry about it.

And maybe I hadn't cried much about everything that had happened to Danny, to me, to the whole stupid world, but I suddenly couldn't keep it back any longer. I kicked the metal gate that someone had drawn across the door, then I started crying hard, harder than I had ever cried. Danny was somewhere in my sobbing, and so were all the animals that had no place to go, had no home, were sold and passed around like funny little creatures we got to control and use for our entertainment. I wanted to break every window in that stupid store, and I even picked up a plastic Rite Aid shopping basket to chuck at the door, but Holly grabbed my arm and pressed it back down.

"It's okay," she said. "Clair, it's okay. There aren't any pets in there now."

She thought I wanted to get inside.

I let her make me drop the basket. Then I sat down on the bench where we used to sit to watch the puppies, and Holly put her arm across my shoulders and let me cry. My nose ran and my ears felt as if someone had set them on fire. I cried until I felt like a hand towel that had been twisted and squeezed to get all the moisture out.

I felt something had changed in the Stewarts' house as soon as we pulled into the driveway after the mall. I hadn't seen much of Elwood since his return except when he left the house for doctor's appointments. I knew it was a slow recovery for him, all beds and raw skin, and it made their house feel haunted.

After Jack and Holly let me out at my back door, I fumbled with my keys, nearly in a panic, and I wanted to call to them to wait as they slowly backed out. I knew my dad wasn't home, and for a tense second I felt stranded and vulnerable, like someone might slap a drugged handkerchief over my mouth and drag me off into the night. A little shock of worry ran up my spine.

I fit the key in finally and pushed into the kitchen, my

heart beating louder than it should. Wally's tail thumped in his crate as I put my bag down, flicked on some lights, then let him out. He smooched me up when I bent down to him, giving me big licks and sitting to give me his paw. I knelt next to him and felt better immediately.

"Who's the best boy?" I asked him. "Who is it?"

He squiggled in my arms until I clipped on his lead. His feet scrambled on the linoleum on the way out. Now that I had lights on, it was pleasant outside. I brought Wally into his place of business and I let him sniff around for a while. He urinated twice, spraying some bushes, then he began growling a little. I turned and saw Elwood watching me from beside the stockade fence. I hadn't heard him approach. He had appeared without making a sound.

"You'll be bringing that dog back in the morning," he said, his voice ugly and flat and hard. "Didn't sign no papers to give him to you. I'm back on my feet now."

He had a thick bandage on his head. You could tell the bandage marked a second stage of his recovery, not the first mummy version, but his face—up around his forehead and around his right eye—had taken on blisters of red that looked like pocked moon soil in the weak light. His skull had been dented too. It looked like it would stay that way.

I tried to feel some sympathy for him, but it didn't come.

Before I could say anything, Wally made a lunge toward him, trying to say hello, and I barely caught his force. I jerked Wally back but I nearly fell. I felt stupid with the dog spazzing.

"Did you hear me?" Elwood asked. "Play time is over. You understand me? I'll expect the dog to be on the pole first thing in the morning."

I nodded. My heart said no, but I nodded.

"You ask me, you drove him to it," Elwood said. "Nothing like a woman to turn a man around and make him stupid."

"You don't want the dog," I managed.

"I don't want you to have it," he said, "and that comes to the same thing. You put it on the pole tomorrow or you won't like what comes to you, believe me. I'm sick to death of you kids. Don't test me."

He turned and left. I watched him walk back toward his house. My brain clouded and I bent down to hug Wally, but I couldn't take my eyes off Elwood.

TWENTY-THREE

LATER, WAITING FOR my father to get home, I made Wally go through his obedience. I practiced him through everything. He did every command immediately, no problems or confusion, and I found myself getting emotional watching him. Twice I bent down and circled his neck with my arms. I buried my face in his neck and cried a little.

"You're a good boy, Wally. A really good boy."

It's what Danny had told him a long time ago.

He rolled over on his back, asking for a belly rub. I petted him a long time. Then I got him up into bed and we rested together, not doing anything, except that I passed his ear slowly through my fingers. I closed my eyes but I knew I wouldn't sleep. My head felt choked with images of Wally and Danny, the car bouncing across the dirt field, the cop yelling *getonthegroundgetontheground*. Sometimes I pictured my mom's statue, the gears turning slowly with the wind, and then I pictured Elwood, too, his black aura, his white bandage holding his skin together. He was a hole, always hungry, always yearning for something and never finding it. I did not like knowing Danny was his son.

A little later Dad came in and I met him downstairs, Wally clattering after me, and I told him what had happened. He had hardly put his helmet down when I started in, and he backed slowly into his chair, his eyes sorting me out. He interrupted me once to ask for a beer, but he kept his attention on me and nodded when I explained things.

"I was afraid of something like this," my dad said when I'd finished. He took a long drink of his beer. He always drank Rolling Rock.

"Like what?" I said, my voice too loud.

"Like this. Like Elwood coming in and wanting something for what he lost. That's why I made you pass on the car."

"He wants Wally!"

"He doesn't want Wally. He just wants you not to have him. Isn't that what he said? There's a difference."

"He's a sicko."

"He might be. That's not a healthy household over there. It never was. You know that."

"I'm not giving him Wally, Dad."

"Just hold on and think it all the way around."

"There's nothing to think about. No way. Wally's not going with that maniac or any of his maniac friends. They'll abuse him. You know they will."

"I'm not disagreeing with you, Clair. Just hold on and think around it. We can talk to him tomorrow. Even if we have to buy Wally, we can buy him. I might be able to reason with him. Maybe Jebby can."

"No, he wants to hurt me, any way he can, Dad. Probably wants to hurt Danny, too."

"Maybe so," Dad said, and shrugged.

I made Dad give Wally a final walk while I watched the Stewarts' house through the kitchen window. I wondered about what was in there, whether anyone had cleaned up the mess Elwood must have made. I wondered if I could talk to Danny and find out what he had told his dad about Wally. My head felt jumpy and empty. My hands shook a little when I ran a glass of water for myself. Dad came back in and let Wally off the leash.

"No sign of the bogeyman," Dad said, draining off the last of his beer.

"It's not funny, Dad. You didn't see how he acted."

"Sorry, honey. I didn't mean to tease."

"Yes, you did."

"Well, I didn't mean it to be mean, I guess is what I want to say. Now come on. Let's turn in. You have to train tomorrow, don't you? The old summer job, right?"

"Yes."

"Okay, we'll talk to him when I get home and you get home. I'll see what Jebby has to say. Jebby knows him a little and he might be able to negotiate something. Just leave Elwood alone for the time being. Keep a wide berth, okay?"

"He said he thinks I made Danny do it. That I was the reason behind it all."

My dad didn't say anything. I saw him flush with anger, but he didn't react right away. He finished his beer. He put his hand down on Wally.

"There is no way on earth you are responsible for anything that happened in that house. Do you understand me, Clair? Whatever happened there was a train going on its own track for a long, long time before you ever got involved. Believe me. He's talking wild. Try not to pay any attention to it. I promise that's not what happened. You know that in your heart."

I hugged my dad. He smelled of oil and gasoline but also of the outdoors and the wind hitting him. He hugged me back. Then I slapped my thigh to put Wally in a heel and ran upstairs with my dog pounding behind me.

That night I had a dream about whippoorwills. Whippoorwills are supposed to witness souls nearing death or departing and they call to them. I pictured one up in the tree between our two yards, its voice singing over and over, *whippoooooorwill, whippppppoooorrrrwillll*. I knew about whippoorwills through a social studies report I had done on early American superstitions, but that little bit of knowledge seeped right into the dream, so that the bird, each time he called, swelled like a tick sucking blood. He kept growing, and growing, plugged with blood and soul juice, until finally he burst and woke me. I sat up and nearly screamed, but then I saw Wally, my Gold Moon, stretched out at the foot of the bed. I reached down to him and cupped his forehead in my hand, and the whippoorwill floated away in Wally's steady breath.

Holly called me at my job twice to check on a boy named Guy, who worked at Joey's Scoops with me and was sort of cute, but not really. They had flirted at a dance, even kissed, but then Guy had started dating a girl named Ellie. Ellie and Guy had dated until the end of the school year, but now Guy was on the market again, and Holly was creeping. She wanted to know what Guy's schedule was, and when I told her I didn't know, she blew a whistle of exasperation.

"You've got to find out," she said. "It's important, Clair."

"He's here now."

"But I can't come down there the first day you get to work. It would be way obvious."

"I have to work, Holly. I have to get off."

"I'll come down later, maybe, if I can convince my jerk-face brother to drive me."

As soon as she hung up, the phone rang again. It was Danny. The I.D. on the phone actually said "Concord Correctional Facility." I looked at Ina, the shift supervisor, and she made a rolling motion with her hand. Take it, but get moving. Ina was nineteen and a sophomore at UNH.

"Sorry," I said to her, then I pushed the button to get Danny.

"Clair?"

"Danny, what are you doing calling?"

"I was able to get a phone out. Long story. I'm getting more privileges. I'm going to be able to call out more often."

"Your dad showed up and wants Wally. He's my dog now. You have to tell him."

"I have told him. That's why I'm calling now. I didn't want you to think I put him up to it."

"Then why's he asking for Wally?"

"He just wants things, Clair. You have to be careful of him. He'll use Wally to hurt you or me. I don't know. He's like that."

"I am not giving Wally to him."

"He thinks he can sell the dog, that's all. Wally, I mean. If he can make ten bucks off him, then that's what he'll do."

"We'll pay him for the dog, if it comes to that."

"He'll hold out for a price. That's the way he is. Be careful of him."

"Listen, I'm at work, Danny."

"Okay, but I can call now. That's what I wanted to say. If that's all right with you, I mean. That's a condition they want to put on it."

"You can call sometimes. Not a lot, I don't think. But sometimes."

"Okay, I will. Did you get my letter about the car?"

"Dad said I can't do that. He said someone would want it. Your father, probably."

"That's what I was going to say anyway. The registration on the car has my dad's name on it too, so I can't give it to you even though I want to. Dad said."

"He visited you?"

"No. We talked on the phone. It was weird."

He didn't say anything. I looked over at Ina, and she gave me a look to tell me to get off the phone. I couldn't imagine what a phone call with a father you tried to kill might be like. I couldn't get my mind around it.

"I have to go, Danny. I'm at work."

"I want you to have Wally. You know that, right?"

"I do, Danny. I'm hanging up now. Stay strong, okay?"

"I will."

I clicked off and slid the phone into my pocket. Ina pointed to the floor and the grill hood. Both needed cleaning.

Father Jasper says all creatures go away from pain and go toward pleasure. Dogs do it and so do humans. It's a simple rule, but it's something you need to remember.

It was raining hard by the time I made it home. Dad was already there, sitting on the porch and doing something with a screwdriver on a piece from his motorcycle. Wally sat beside him, his lead tied to my dad's chair. I bent down and kissed Wally's nose. The rain smelled good and it sounded nice coming off the roof. Dad had a cup of tea beside him. It was still warm enough to steam.

"I talked with Elwood," he said when I finished with

Wally. "He was out in the yard and I went over and had a talk with him."

"And what did he say?"

"He's pulling out all the scrap metal in the back. The old tractors and such. The price of metal is up, even for old buckets like those tractors. He's cleaning the place up to sell it. He's still in pretty horrible shape. I don't think his face is ever going to be right again."

"What about Wally, Dad?"

"He wants a thousand dollars."

"What? You're kidding me, right?"

My dad looked at me. He didn't need to explain that he didn't have a thousand dollars hanging around.

"It's probably just a bargaining ploy. He wants to set the price way up and see how high we'll jump. He doesn't want the dog, I don't think."

"What a terrible man. He just wants to hurt me or Danny or even Wally."

"I agree, Clair, but he has us over a barrel. He does. It's his dog, technically."

"Tell him to prove it."

"He could if he needed to. He could get neighbors to testify. Now, don't misunderstand me. We're going to make sure Wally stays with us, but in the meantime we probably need to tie him out again."

"I'm not doing that."

He looked at me. He looked tired and scared. Scared that I would hate him, scared that he let me down. I felt bad for him, but I didn't care. Wally was my only concern.

"I'll make him a counteroffer. Say five hundred. He's not going to get more than that from anyone else. I'll offer cash money and he'll think about it and then he'll say yes. That's the way these guys work. He's all bluff."

"No, he's not," I said, because I knew he wasn't.

"No offense, Wally," Dad said, petting Wally's neck, "but he is not worth five hundred even. He's not, Clair. He might be to us, but not to anyone else."

"If you offer five hundred, he'll hold out for a thousand. Or he'll give Wally away for spite. He will. I don't know how I know it, but I do."

"He may not be as bad as you think, Clair. He's greedy, that's all."

"He's more than greedy. He deserved what he got from Danny. You said so yourself."

"Well, that's the way it sits right now. He said we could wait until you got home."

"He wants to tie him out now, in the rain?"

Dad didn't say anything. His head moved a fraction of an inch to say yes.

TWENTY-FOUR

NOW IT WAS CRUELER. Wally knew what it was like inside, knew what it was to be loved, to be warm and out of the elements. I heard him outside, whining, his chain occasionally clinking. I couldn't stand it. I put cotton in my ears and tried to drown it out with music, but nothing worked. I knew where Wally was, and he knew where I was, and leaving him out like that made my heart empty.

Dad had taken him over to the Stewarts'. He had offered to keep Wally, just on loan, as it were, but Elwood refused, stating that he was the sort to have things lined up. He liked order. He pointed out that he might have a customer for Wally, and then where would he be? The customer wouldn't be able to see the dog because it was in our house, and that wouldn't work, would it? No, he concluded, better to let the dog stay out and get accustomed to his house again. Besides, he added, the weather was no longer a problem for the foreseeable future.

The entire conversation turned my blood to acid. I worried that he would simply get rid of Wally or take him out and shoot him. I wouldn't put it past him.

But I'll admit this: I was afraid of Elwood. As much as I loved Wally, I still couldn't bring myself to go over and get him. It was like it had been earlier when I was too lazy, or too bored, or too self-involved, to take a stand and get Wally in the first place. I hated that about myself, but it was a streak I couldn't deny.

I had so much cotton in my ears, and the music was so loud, that I didn't hear my dad knock. Finally he pushed the door open and I shrieked.

"Sorry, sorry, sorry," he said, holding up his hand. "Sorry to barge in, but I knocked and you didn't answer."

"I'm trying not to hear Wally," I said, and turned down the music.

"I came up to tell you that I'm running over to Jebby's. I won't be long, but I don't want you to go over to Wally. Do you understand me?"

I nodded.

"I mean it, Clair. You won't improve the situation by annoying Elwood. He's a dangerous man. I know how you feel, but the dog belongs to him."

"Bull."

"By law."

"Go ahead," I said, giving in. "I won't harass him."

"He's not someone I trust."

"Join the club."

"Just leave him alone. I have your word, right?"

I nodded again.

"I'm sorry about all this, Clair. I am."

"I know. Seems like people always take from us, though. It's never the other way around. You ever notice that?"

Dad gazed at me an unusually long time, finally shrugged, then pulled the door shut. I turned the music back up, but it bored me. I switched to an old *Law & Order* on my computer, and I put the headphones over my ears. I heard Dad's Harley splatter away.

My phone vibrated a little later and it was Holly. She still wanted to know about Guy and whether I thought he was over Ellie. I told Holly I had no clue, no way to know, that she should ask him herself. She wondered too if they had had sex. She had heard a rumor that they had, but it wasn't confirmed. I didn't get into it with her.

"What are you all gloomy about?" she asked.

I told her about Wally. She knew most of it already, but she didn't know the latest development.

"That sucks," she said. "I know how much you love that dog, Clair."

"Sometimes it feels like everything just drops away from me and my dad. Like we can't hold on to anything, not even a stupid dog. Wally is right back where he started, and Mr. Stewart may just kill him. Just to be horrible. The thing is, Wally would think he was playing right up to the moment he killed him. That's what I can't stand. He would think you were playing if you put a gun to his head."

"Oh, jeez, Clair."

I let her change the topic and we talked about her two monster girls, the ones she took care of as a nanny, and she told a few stories about the girls' mom and how terrible she was. She said the mom ate celery sticks and Marshmallow Fluff and gave them to the girls, too. She called them Angel Wings. The girls loved them. The girls always had Fluff lines around their lips and on their fingers.

"You okay?" she asked before we hung up. "You want me to come over or something?"

"No, it's okay. I have to work tomorrow."

"You could come over here, Clair. Just to get away from hearing Wally."

"I want to hear him."

I didn't know if that was the truth, but I let it stand.

"I wish I could do something to help," Holly said.

"You're my friend. That helps."

"I'm glad," she said, and hung up after a few more minutes.

After that I got ready for bed. I washed my face and put on some Noxzema to dry up a zit I was getting on my chin, then I climbed into bed and did nothing for a while. I didn't hear Wally and that put me into a panic. I kept the lights off and walked to the window and looked down to see him. I thought of Danny and I thought of that first time I had really seen them together, and my insides felt like they might cave down into a lump in my stomach and stay there forever.

It took a long time for my eyes to adjust, but eventually I saw Wally. He lay on the ground beside the house, his chin resting on his paws. Light barely found him. When he moved his head to bite at a bug, the chain made a sound like it had in the old days. He was waiting, I knew. He was waiting for me or for anyone else who wanted to show him kindness. He didn't judge that no one came by, though I knew his heart must have been broken. He simply waited, not expecting much, never counting on anything.

I heard it a long way off.

It came like buffalo running. I sat up in bed and I

knew the sound but I couldn't place it at first. Then my heart filled. It filled in a torrent and sleep slid away like ice shedding from a roof. I pulled on my clothes as fast as I could and the sound kept building. It grew to every space, filled it like foam or water, and then it was the only thing, the whole world vibrating.

I ran downstairs and the sound grew bigger and bigger and I went out on the porch. The rain from earlier had disappeared and now the air hung cool and crisp and moist. I heard them coming, a hundred motorcycles, two hundred, and they rode hard, gunning, and I started to cry. Because I knew where they were headed, knew why they were coming, and they weren't the Hells Angels or anything as tough, but they were coming to help me and I knew it. Maybe it was a small thing, not a big rally or a fight against social injustice, but my dad had saddled them up, called in all favors, every last one for his daughter, and I could feel the boom in my gut.

Then they came down our street. If you've never heard a couple hundred Harleys running full bore, then you can't imagine it. The windowpanes in our old windows chattered. The trees shook. Lights came on everywhere. And then they rolled up onto the Stewarts' lawn, their bikes hissing and loud, the engines sucking everything out of the air. They pointed their noses at the Stewarts' house, shining light on the cockroach named Elwood, and I saw my dad dismount and wave to me and I knew what he wanted.

Dad kissed my cheek, yelled into my ear, and he nodded when we both understood.

I ran to get Wally. I knelt beside him, and I saw his eye was swollen shut with blood, and his lip was fat and misshapen. Someone had kicked him, no doubt Elwood. I kissed his stupid head and held him for a second, then I grabbed him off his line and brought him with me. He couldn't hear a thing and the motorcycles, the lights, made him crazy, but I brought him and put him in my dad's pickup and I backed out with an escort of a couple hundred Harleys. I rolled down my window to spit at the Stewarts' property, at Elwood, because he could not have my dog, would never have my dog, and that was all there was to it. I drove carefully, not sure where all the bikes were, and I saw Jebby with his rhino head, and a few other men I knew, and they all nodded. And you had to laugh —this great commotion over a dog, and how silly it was to have a motorcycle gang with no more toughness than to liberate a neighborhood hound—but it had given them something to do and they looked happy and solemn and proud of themselves. I held out my hand and waved and they gunned up after me, falling into position, and I had my own phalanx of Harley men, more than I could see, all of them getting their bikes to blat and shiver and cause people to sit up in their beds.

I put my arm around Wally and I drove. We went out of that neighborhood and onto the open highway, and one after another of the Harley boys whizzed past, saying goodbye, and I blew them kisses and cried and told Wally someone in this stupid, stupid world cared after all.

TWENTY-FIVE

I ARRIVED AT the Maine Academy for Dogs at first light. I was alone with Wally. My dad had dropped away after a conversation at a rest stop, and he had given me a hundred dollars and accepted my plan. I kissed him and said I'd be home later. I said it was something I had to do myself. Then I had driven through the night to Fryeburg, Maine.

It was pretty. And I don't know why, but it reminded me of my mom, of her statue, and I wondered what she had thought out on the road alone. Your mind could do crazy things when you were in a car alone, but I had Wally. If she had had Wally, a dog, a small second heart beating with hers, I wondered if the end would have come for her. I didn't think so.

I found a man walking a German shepherd beside the road. I slowed down and pulled over. Morning light turned the grass of the academy gray and white where the dew still covered it.

"Just up on your right," the man said when I explained my situation. "Follow the signs for visitors. Look for a white building with a granite chimney."

He looked like anyone else except for a sweatshirt that said MAINE ACADEMY FOR DOGS across his chest. His dog sat beside him without moving a whisker.

"See that?" I told Wally when we moved off. "You see what you can be?"

Wally's tongue hung out of his mouth, and he shifted his weight whenever we took a turn.

There was no one at the white house with the granite chimney. It was too early. I parked in the shade of a catalpa tree and took Wally out for a walk. He urinated in five or six places. When he finished, I bent down and examined his face. His eye probably required medical attention. I couldn't say for certain.

An older man approached as I stood up from examining Wally. I knew at a glance that it was Father Jasper.

His beard, half grown in, was pure white. His eyes looked soft and hazy, but they held an inner light. He was old, profoundly old. He reminded me of a turtle, a quiet old creature making his way in the world without disturbing anyone else. He looked clean and happy, calm in a way that made me relax to see him. He smiled. He held out his hand knuckles-first to let Wally sniff him. He didn't seem to think it was odd to find a girl with a dog waiting for him in the early morning.

"What a nice dog," he said, his voice quiet in the morning air. "What's happened to him? Looks like he had an accident."

"Someone kicked him. Hit him, anyway."

"Oh, that's horrible. You poor boy. Is he all right otherwise?"

"I think so."

"Have you removed him from that situation?"

"Yes."

"Good for you. It's always a terrible thing to see someone be unkind to a pet or any animal for that matter. There's a victim on each side of the beating. So sad."

"Are you . . . ?" I asked, not sure what I wanted to say.

"Father Jasper?" he finished for me, and gently laughed. "Guilty. I'm the crazy dog lover. And this, as you can see, is the academy the dogs built for themselves."

"I used your book to train him."

"Did you? And how did that work? Did you find the book useful?"

I liked his voice. I liked it very much.

"It was extremely useful. He's a good boy now. He was wild when I first started with him. That book changed him."

"Did you do it alone?"

"Mostly. A friend named Danny helped me."

"I see."

Then I told him the whole story. I don't know why. I don't know why he listened, but he seemed to expect that I wanted to tell him something and he was a priest when all was said and done. The story came out like a piece of tape uncurling from my mouth. At one point he lowered the tailgate on our pickup and sat. He listened carefully, his hand sometimes petting Wally. No one else was around. Morning was still just coming over the mountains.

"That's quite a story," he said when I finished. "You've been through a lot and so has Wally here. Would you show me how he's done? I'd like to see his training."

I bent down to Wally and kissed his head, then I put him through his obedience. My heart filled with pride. He may not have been at the top of his game because of his injuries, but he did his best and did it cheerfully, and Father

Jasper smiled a great deal watching him. Wally was not a purebred dog, and he had spent most of his life as a piece of junk, but he did his best and I felt proud as anything, proud as I had ever been.

"Well, he's a good boy, isn't he?" Father Jasper said. "You've worked hard with him, haven't you? I can see that. He's well behaved. He's a good dog citizen."

I nodded. My eyes filled. That was a high praise coming from Father Jasper. It meant everything to me.

"Is there a place," I asked, when I thought I could control my voice, "where he could go to be safe?"

"You want to put him into our protection?"

I nodded. Father Jasper thought for a moment.

"He's an old dog, you understand. Probably past his mid years, but we could place him with a good family. I know of one that might be perfect for him. Is that what you want?"

I nodded. I looked down at Wally. His good eye looked back at me, and I felt my heart crumble.

"You're afraid to bring him back to where he was? Is that so?"

"Yes. That man I mentioned will keep trying to get him, to hurt him, and I'm not sure we can prevent that."

"I'm so sorry."

"You'll make sure it's a good home, won't you? With

kids, maybe. He'd like someone to play with. He didn't have anyone to play with for a long time."

I couldn't help it. I started to cry harder.

"It's a very good home with excellent dog owners. He couldn't do better, but do you want to think about this at all?" he asked. "Give it some time?"

I shook my head. I tried to talk but I couldn't.

"You have thought about it, haven't you?" he asked gently. "Why else would you show up here? This is a great act of mercy, Clair. Yes, we could take him if you're certain. That's part of our mission too."

I handed the lead to Father Jasper. He accepted it. It meant a lot giving the lead to Father Jasper. To the author of *My Pack*. To a man who used dogs to keep him whole and to lead him to heaven.

I bent down and hugged Wally. I held him a long time. I whispered in his ear that he was the best boy, a good boy, my Gold Moon. I kissed his bad eye lightly, and I saw the sun reflecting off his coat. I told him he had come home at last, that he was free, that he was a dog even Father Jasper had to admire. Then I stood up.

"You've demonstrated great love," Father Jasper said. "And I admire you for it. I will make Wally my own special project and keep him safe the rest of his days. You have my word."

I nodded and went back to the truck. It was still early morning. I watched Father Jasper walk slowly away with Wally in a perfect heel, both of them in silhouette from the sunlight, Wally's head turned up to see what was expected, what was hoped, what might be.

JOSEPH MONNINGER is an English professor and New Hampshire tour guide. He is the author of the young adult novels *Finding Somewhere, Wish, Hippie Chick,* and *Baby.* He also writes fiction and nonfiction for adults. He lives in Warren, New Hampshire.